# THE SURVIVAL RULE

## A RAIN CITY LEGAL THRILLER

## STEPHEN PENNER

D0869449

**INKUBATOR**
**BOOKS**

Published by Inkubator Books
www.inkubatorbooks.com

ISBN (eBook): 978-1-83756-292-3
ISBN (Paperback): 978-1-83756-293-0
ISBN (Hardback): 978-1-83756-294-7

# 1

———

"Choose your next words very carefully, Mr. Raine."

The judge scowled down from his bench, gavel in hand, ready—perhaps even eager—to hold attorney Daniel Raine in contempt of court. There could be a fine line between zealous advocacy and punishable misconduct. Especially when the judge was Judge Norton Carruthers, the oldest judge in the county. And especially when the client was Jimmy "Bam Bam" Galloway. Galloway had committed a lot of crimes in his short lifetime. But he hadn't committed the one he was on trial for that day.

It was time for Raine to strike a blow for the independence of the bar. And for the innocence of his client.

"Isn't it true, Mr. Beecham," Raine went ahead and asked the question Judge Carruthers had warned him against, "that you are a confidential informant for the Seattle Police Department? And further, that you fed them false information about Mr. Galloway in order to regain your good standing with them after being caught selling drugs to minors?"

Galloway had told Raine, insisted even, that Beecham was an informant, but he didn't have any evidence. The prosecutor had objected to raising the issue in front of the jury without proof, even though she could have easily confirmed whether Beecham was a snitch. Without the evidence the prosecutor refused to hand over to support Galloway's assertion, the judge had ordered Raine not to ask about it. "Lack of foundation," the judge had ruled. But Beecham was the star witness against Galloway. If Raine didn't reveal to the jury that Beecham had a reason to lie and did lie to the cops, then the jurors would believe him, and Raine's client would go to prison for a crime he didn't commit. It was an easy decision for Raine.

"Objection!" the prosecutor shouted.

"I warned you, Mr. Raine!" the judge boomed.

Raine ignored both of them. He picked up a raft of papers from his table and shook them at Beecham. "I've got the receipts, Carl. Don't add perjury to the list of offenses you're going to have to work off."

It was a bluff. The papers had nothing to do with Beecham.

"Objection!" the prosecutor repeated.

"Mr. Raine!" the judge repeated as well.

"Yes," Beecham answered amid the cacophony. It was almost a whisper, but everyone heard it. "Yes, I'm a C.I. for the cops. And yes, I lied about Bam Bam."

That silenced the prosecutor. And the judge.

"Did Mr. Galloway commit the crime?" Raine put the finest point he could on it. "Or did you lie to save your own hide?"

Beecham sighed and dropped his head. "I lied."

A murmur pulsed through the jury box. The trial was over, for all intents and purposes.

"Thank you for your honesty, Mr. Beecham." Raine nodded to the witness. "No further questions."

The courtroom sat in stunned silence for several seconds.

Then Judge Carruthers looked down at the prosecutor. "Ms. Kilpatrick, do you have a motion?"

Kilpatrick could have asked the judge to sustain her objection and strike Beecham's testimony. That would involve the judge telling the jurors to disregard what Beecham had said. But trial lawyers had a saying: you can't unring a bell.

"Yes, Your Honor." The prosecutor sighed. "The State moves to dismiss."

---

"AND THAT'S how you win a case, baby!" Raine burst into his office and pointed a triumphant finger at his receptionist/secretary/paralegal and only employee, Laura Johnston. "You seek justice no matter the personal cost."

Raine was expecting a "Heck yeah!" sort of response from Laura, but instead she smiled weakly and pointed to the chairs behind the door. He turned and saw for the first time the man seated there. He was young and solidly built, with thick forearms and sandy hair. His clothes were casual but expensive-looking. His watch probably cost more than Raine's car.

He stood up and extended a hand. He was almost as tall as Raine's six feet three inches, with thicker forearms and an iron grip. "I knew I'd come to the right place. J. Daniel Raine, attorney at law, I presume?"

Raine shook the man's hand. "Dan is fine," he assured his guest. "Can I help you with a legal matter?"

"I sure hope so," the man answered. "I'm Adam Harper. Of Harper Development. And I want you to help me spring your biggest trap yet."

Raine liked the sound of that. Big meant expensive, which meant money to keep the lights on and Laura paid. Raine had seen the "Harper Development" signs hanging outside construction sites all over town. There always seemed to be a new skyscraper going up somewhere in downtown Seattle, and Harper Development seemed to be attached to at least a quarter of those projects, maybe more. Raine hadn't had a reason to pay close attention to the exact numbers, but he'd seen enough to know Adam Harper of Harper Development was going to be able to pay for that big trap he wanted. And Raine was curious who the trap was for.

Raine instructed Laura to hold his calls and knew he could trust her not to reply with a comment of how infrequently the phone rang. Being a solo practitioner could mean long, lean times between the occasional, but all too infrequent, lucrative clients. They both needed Raine to sign up Adam Harper.

"Right this way, Mr. Harper." Raine gestured toward his office. "Let's see how I can help you."

As they walked down the hall, Raine couldn't help but try to guess what this was about. A dispute with a subcontractor? Problems securing the proper zoning permits? An injured worker? The possibilities were almost endless for a business engaged in the high-risk, high-reward world of real estate development and construction.

Raine entered his office and bid Adam to sit across his desk from him. Raine followed suit and clasped his hands in front of him. "What can I do for you, Mr. Harper?"

"I want to sue my father," Adam answered.

Raine's eyebrows shot up. Endless possibilities indeed.

"I want to take the company away from him," Adam expounded. "He's old, and he's going senile. We're in the middle of our largest project ever, the Harper Tower. Named after our company, our family. Sixty stories of retail and residential right downtown at Fifth and Seneca. The tallest condo tower in the city. My dad calls it his 'monument to the sky'. But it will fail if my dad stays in charge of the company. Someone needs to push him out before it's too late."

"And you're that someone?" Raine surmised.

"My brother won't do it," Adam answered. "And there's no one else in the family. My dad built the company literally from the ground up, but I'll be damned if I'm going to just stand by and watch it all fall back to earth."

Raine lowered his hands onto his desk and nodded thoughtfully. "Okay, I'm going to need some more details. First of all, what's your dad's name?"

"William Harper," Adam answered. "He goes by Bill."

"Bill Harper." Raine tried the name on. "Now, what about corporate structure? Who owns what?"

"It's a closely held corporation," he said. "Dad owns seventy percent of the stock. My brother, Mark, and I each own fifteen percent. Even if we combined our votes, we would have less than half of Dad's share. He set it up that way. But it doesn't matter. Mark will never move against my dad. He's too scared of him. He calls it loyalty, but it's really fear. I went to him first. I thought maybe we could talk to Dad, make him see that it's time to let go of the company. But

Mark refused. He refuses to see what's happening. I told him if we didn't do anything, then we'd both own fifteen percent of nothing."

"Or worse," Raine pointed out. "Fifteen percent of the outstanding debts of a bankrupt company."

"Exactly!" Adam pointed a finger at Raine. "I knew you'd understand."

Raine understood the dangers of bankruptcy. Adam Harper was going to help him avoid it for another month. If there was anything to his claims.

"Why do you think your dad is so senile he can't run the business anymore?" Raine asked. "Forgetting the grandkids' birthdays or putting his car keys in the refrigerator isn't going to cut it. It needs to be more than just forgetfulness, and it needs to be business related. It needs to be substantial and provable."

Adam nodded. "I understand. As you can imagine, it didn't just start out of nowhere. He's not that old, only seventy-one, but there have been signs. Little things. Ignoring emails. Missing meetings. General confusion. But then it started getting worse. Things that actually impact the project. He's started making decisions that he would never have made before, and it's jeopardizing everything."

"Like what?" Raine asked.

"Like firing our HVAC subcontractor," Adam answered, "with no replacement company lined up. We've used the same HVAC company for over a decade. They know what we want, and we know they can do it. But then Dad just terminated the contract and is refusing to pay for any work they already did. They're going to sue us, and they're going to win. In the meantime, we can't proceed with construction until we get a new HVAC company on board. You can't just add that stuff at the end. It's integral to every room on every floor.

"That means we have workers with nothing to do. Everyone in this industry understands there are delays sometimes. But we can't pay the workers not to do anything, and they can't sit around not getting paid for very long. They have families to feed just like everyone else. We're already getting heat from the union boss, and we don't need that, I can tell you."

"Is it just that one subcontractor?" Raine inquired.

"No, it's more than that," Adam answered. "So much more. For example, we should have already been lining up tenants for the retail on the lower floors, but Dad is refusing. He says we'll be able to charge twice as much once everyone sees how beautiful his sky monument is."

"Is he right?" Raine asked. That seemed like a possibly sound business decision.

"No, he's senile," Adam insisted. "It's an office tower, not the Taj Mahal. Sure, it'll be pretty. All glass and steel and reflecting the water and the mountain, but every building in Seattle does that too. It's real estate, not an art exhibition. That means it's about three things: location, location, and location. We've already been approached by some very large and exclusive retailers, but Dad has turned them all away. If we have no tenants lined up when we complete construction, that's months and months of lost rental revenue."

"Which you might never get if your father keeps firing subcontractors and not paying union workers," Raine pointed out.

Another approving gesture across the desk at Raine. "Exactly."

"Okay." Raine accepted the information Adam had

provided. Then he posed his final questions, perhaps the most important. "Who else knows you're here? Who will try to stop you?"

"Dad will definitely try to stop me." Adam chuckled darkly. "But he doesn't know I'm here."

"What about your brother?"

"He knows what I want to do," Adam answered. "Like I said, I went to him first. But he doesn't know I'm here. He just wants to put his head in the sand and pretend it's all going to go away."

"Will he try to stop us?" Raine needed to know who they would be up against.

Adam shook his head. "I don't think so. If we win, he'll be relieved."

"When we win," Raine corrected. It was marketing, but it was important to display confidence to a new client. Especially right before talking about the fee. "But it's not going to be easy—"

"And that means it's not going to be cheap," Adam finished Raine's thought. "I know. That's why I tracked you down. I wanted someone hungry, but also good. I asked around, and you have a solid reputation as a fighter and a winner."

Raine was glad to hear that.

"Plus, our firm has used pretty much every large- and medium-sized law firm in Seattle over the last decade," Adam continued, "so they're all conflicted out. I needed someone we never would have thought of hiring before."

Raine was less glad to hear that. But he wasn't the type to pick a fight with reality.

"So will you take the case?" Adam asked.

Raine was tempted to agree to it right then and there.

The case promised to be both complicated and contested. That meant a lot of billable hours. Even if he ultimately lost, he'd make a lot of money along the way. Unless he got absolutely crushed right out of the gate. That could lead to bad publicity, a diminished reputation, and an unhappy client who wouldn't want to pay his bills. No one likes paying to lose.

Raine knew he was only getting one side of the story. That was the nature of a new client consultation. Before he jumped into a lawsuit against one of the richest developers in the city, Raine wanted the other side of the story.

"Probably," he answered. "But first, I want to consult with my expert."

"**E**xpert?" Rebecca Sommers laughed at the characterization. "Oh, Dan. I'm flattered."

Raine had come to Sommers's office to ask her what she knew about Harper Development and specifically Adam Harper and his father. He explained what Adam wanted him to do and why, and that he had left him hanging to consult with his "expert".

"You're one of the top real estate agents in the city," Raine began his explanation.

"The number one commercial real estate agent in Seattle, downtown core and First Hill," Sommers reminded him. She looked the part. Long, lush, platinum hair. Expertly applied makeup. Precious stones flashing from a collection of rings and bracelets. Perfectly tailored silk suit.

"Exactly," Raine responded. "You must know these Harpers and whether I'll be walking into a buzzsaw if I take the case."

Sommers steepled her fingers and turned her chair to look out the floor-to-ceiling windows at her view of Mount

Rainier. They were on the twentieth floor of one of the smaller office towers in the lower financial district, several blocks north of Raine's own one-story office building on the edge of the International District. She shared the floor with several other professionals, but her office was her own, and it reflected its occupant. Classy, expensive, successful. Exactly what her clients would want to see when they walked in.

"I do, and you will," Sommers answered. She spun back around to face him. "But that doesn't mean you shouldn't take the case."

Raine smiled slightly. That had been his impression too.

"Harper Development is the biggest residential condo developer in the city. The state, actually," Sommers corrected. "Probably three or four states. And everybody knows Bill Harper. He does mostly residential, and I do mostly commercial, so I've never interacted with him directly, but you hear things."

"What kind of things?" This was exactly the intel Raine needed to make his decision about taking on Adam's case.

"He's smart," Sommers said. "And ruthless. If you're his friend, he'll do anything for you, but he only has a few friends. And if you're his enemy, well, you'd better watch out. He knows what he wants, he knows how to get it, and he always does. You don't want to be in his way."

"Sounds like a formidable foe," Raine observed. "Does he also give millions to charity and take sick kids to the circus?"

"Oh, no, definitely not." Sommers laughed. "He loves his money, and he's not about to give it away. He pays bottom dollar and charges top dollar. He busts unions and fires anyone who disagrees with him."

"How is that a successful business model?" Raine wondered.

"Bottom dollar for a billion-dollar project is still a lot of dollars," Sommers pointed out. "If you don't take the subcontract, your competitor will. But you have to be careful. And this is the part you need to pay attention to."

Raine leaned forward slightly. "What's that?"

"He has a reputation for not paying his bills," Sommers warned. "Basically he's a bully who doesn't pay if he thinks he can get away with it. So be careful."

"You think his kid will try to do the same to me?" Raine asked.

Sommers shrugged. "I don't know. Some apples don't fall far from the tree. I would just be sure to get paid up front. And maybe add a surcharge in case you don't get your last invoice paid."

Raine leaned back in his chair and considered. "Do you think there's anything to Adam's claims? Could his dad really be losing it?"

Sommers rubbed her chin. "Maybe. He's not that old. Seventy, maybe? But everybody's different. It could be that the old man is losing it. Or it could be that his kid is just an asshole."

They both thought for a moment, then said in unison, "Probably both."

They both laughed, then Sommers asked, "So, are you going to take the case?"

"A questionable case against a cutthroat bully?" Raine asked. "With hundreds of millions of dollars on the line, both sides are probably assholes, and I might have to sue my own client at the end just to get paid?" He grinned broadly. "Rebecca, my dear, a case like this is why I became a lawyer."

"Then you should take the case, my dear Daniel."

Raine stood up and clapped his hands together. "Thank you for your expert advice. I'm off to sign up my new client."

Sommers stood up too. "I'll come with you," she offered.

"For moral support?"

Sommers laughed. "No, of course not. I want to see how far along this development is. Maybe I can get in on some action, rent some of those retail spaces."

"Adam said his dad hasn't started looking for tenants yet," Raine reminded her.

"And I just advised you to take the case so his son could start doing that," Sommers pointed out. "What a coincidence."

## 3

The construction site for the future Harper Tower stretched over the entire block between Fifth and Sixth Avenues and Seneca and Spring Streets. It was surrounded by a tall wire fence and multiple signs warning that only authorized personnel outfitted in proper safety equipment could enter. But Raine was a lawyer. Lawyers lived between the rules.

Sommers shaded her eyes as she looked up at the rising steel scaffolding. "Looks like it's really coming along. They're going to have an amazing view. Too bad we can't get inside."

"Who says we can't?" Raine grinned.

Sommers lowered her gaze to her companion, then jerked a thumb at the nearest "AUTHORIZED PERSONNEL ONLY" sign. "That sign. And a dozen more like it."

Raine shook his head. "It doesn't apply to us."

Sommers put a fist on her hip and took an exaggerated stance as she read the sign again. "I'm pretty sure it does, Dan."

"Let me phrase it differently," Raine allowed. "If they

were city signs, they would apply to everyone. However, this is a private job site, and those signs were put up by the company, so they can be selectively enforced. They only apply to people the company says they apply to. And I know one of the owners."

Sommers twisted her lips into a knot. "I think OSHA might disagree with you."

Raine pulled open the gate in the fence. "Fine. We'll put on hard hats when we get inside. Happy now?"

Sommers placed a finger under Raine's chin as she slipped past him into the construction site. "You'll know when I'm not happy, Dan."

Raine had no doubt about that. He followed her and pulled the gate shut behind them.

"Hey! You two!" the nearest worker yelled. "What are you doing in here? This is a restricted area!"

Apparently a man in a suit and a woman in heels were obviously out of place on a construction site.

"Told you so," Sommers whispered out of the corner of her mouth.

"It's okay." Raine raised his hands at the fast-approaching worker. "I'm a lawyer."

"Oh, for God's sake," Sommers muttered, very much not under her breath. "With the city," she appended. "We're here to speak with Adam Harper."

The worker stopped in his tracks. "Is there a problem?"

"Not if you go fetch Mr. Harper," Sommers answered. She looked up at the half-finished building towering above them. "And get us a couple of hard hats."

The worker hesitated, then nodded profusely and scrambled away, first to provide them each with a hard hat, then, presumably, to find Adam Harper.

"Why did you say that?" Raine asked. "I don't work for the city."

"I didn't say you worked for the city," Sommers answered. "I said you were 'with' the city. And you're with the city, aren't you? You're not against it, right?"

Raine could only shake his head. "Yes, I am very much for the city."

"With," Sommers corrected. "And I doubt Adam wants anyone here to know that he's consulted with a lawyer. Do you know why everyone hates lawyers?"

"Jealousy?" Raine offered.

"No," Sommers replied forcefully. "People hate lawyers because lawyers only show up when bad things have happened, or are about to happen. If people know Adam has hired you, they will immediately wonder why and start talking. Bill Harper will know what Adam has planned before we turn in our hard hats."

Raine frowned, but he couldn't disagree. And Adam confirmed Sommers's theory when he stormed up to them.

"What are you doing here?" he demanded. "My father can't know about this." He noticed Sommers. "And who is this?"

"I'm his expert," Sommers answered.

"My investigator," Raine corrected. "This is Rebecca Sommers."

She extended her hand. "I'm also an expert."

Adam shook Sommers's hand. "Okay. If you say so." He glanced around furtively, then nodded toward the trailer nearby. "Come on. Let's go inside. I don't want to be seen out here with you. People will start talking, if they haven't already."

Raine followed Sommers and Adam into the trailer.

There was a single worker inside whom Adam promptly sent away on a pretextual errand. Then Adam showed them into the semi-private office portion of the trailer and sat down behind a small desk. Raine and Sommers sat in the only other two chairs in the room. Raine took off his hard hat. Sommers touched hers admiringly and left it on.

"Okay, why are you here, Raine?" Adam demanded. "Are you going to take the case?"

"I am," Raine answered. "And that's exactly why I'm here." He reached into his coat pocket and extracted the fee agreement he had picked up from Laura on the drive over. "I just need you to sign this. And provide the deposit for the retainer."

Adam took the document and frowned. "How much is the retainer?"

Raine looked briefly to Sommers, who raised an eyebrow at him, clearly to remind him of her previous warning. "Twenty-five thousand."

Adam's head jerked up from his perusal of the fee agreement. "That seems like a lot. What's your hourly rate?"

"It is a lot," Raine answered. He nodded at the papers in Adam's hands. "The rates are all spelled out in the agreement. I expect this to be a highly contested litigation. Unless you think your father is just going to hand the company over to you."

"If I thought that," Adam answered, "I wouldn't have hired you."

He frowned again, but then pulled open a drawer and extracted a pen and a check register. He reviewed the fee agreement, signed it, then opened the register and started filling out the check. "It won't take Dad long to notice this check. And there's probably somebody already on his way up to tell him about the lawyer, and his expert, who showed up to talk to me. You need to file the case as soon as possible."

"I usually prefer to do a little research before I file a multimillion-dollar litigation," Raine replied.

But Adam shook his head. "There's no time. As soon as Dad figures out what's happening, he'll move to push me out of the company. We need to file this while I'm still a shareholder."

"How can he do that?" Sommers questioned.

"He'll figure out a way," Adam assured.

Raine paused for a moment. "I thought you said he was going senile. Suddenly, he's sharp enough to figure out how to push you out of the company before I file a lawsuit he doesn't even know about yet?"

"That's what I was going to ask," Sommers concurred.

Adam frowned and shook his hands in a frustrated gesture. "He's in and out, okay? Sometimes he can't remember the name of the project or what year it is. Other times, he's aware of everything everyone around him is doing. And anyway, he's paranoid all of the time. Whether he's in his right mind or not, he's going to think I'm up to something."

"And he would be right," Sommers acknowledged.

"So just file the case," Adam exhorted. "As soon as possible. First thing tomorrow morning, if you can."

Raine wasn't going to move quite that fast. The check wouldn't have cleared by then. But he assured his client that he would start the litigation as expeditiously as possible. "Tomorrow morning won't work, but I think I can get it filed by the next day. Let's make that the target."

The frown Adam had been wearing since first

approaching them only deepened. "I guess so. If you say so. I think I can avoid him until then."

"Avoid your brother too," Raine advised. "And anyone associated with the company. Go on a fishing trip or something."

"I hate fishing," Adam replied. "Dad always used to take us on fishing trips when we were kids. We both hated it, but Mark always pretended he loved it. Anything to make Dad happy."

"Mark is going to be a problem," Sommers opined.

"Bill is going to be the biggest problem," Raine replied, "and his lawyers, whoever they end up being."

"They'll be the best," Adam said. "I can tell you that much."

Sommers patted Raine on the arm. "Second best," she insisted.

Raine shook his head at the compliment. "Let's just get this case filed. Then we'll see who the best lawyer is."

## 4

Two days later, the check had cleared, and the pleadings were drafted.

Raine printed out three copies each of the summons and complaint, the documents necessary to commence a civil lawsuit, and departed his office for the King County Courthouse a few blocks away. One copy was for the court, one copy was for his file, and one copy was for Bill Harper and whoever his lawyers ended up being. He would date-stamp all three to prove when he had filed it, and to show his as-yet-to-be-determined opposing counsel that he was serious. He wasn't wasting time with a demand letter and a threat to file suit. He had already filed it. It wasn't like a demand letter was going to work anyway. By all accounts, Bill Harper wasn't going to hand over control of the company he'd built from the ground up just because someone asked.

Raine was looking forward to getting the paperwork filed and handing off a copy to the process server to track down Bill Harper and shove the lawsuit in his hand. But apparently, he was going to have to wait a few more minutes. When he arrived at the clerk's office, he found a line. A short line—only one person—but the tone of the conversation between that one person and the clerk suggested it might take a while.

"I understand what a local rule is, honey," the woman in line was saying. "What I don't understand is why you don't understand what the rule actually says."

The woman had been leaning on the clerk's counter but stood up and seemed to sense Raine's approach. She turned around and faced him.

He'd never seen her before. He was sure of that. He never would have forgotten her. She was tall, probably close to six feet, with short blonde hair, thick black eyebrows, and full red lips. Elaborate earrings hung almost to the shoulders of her sharply tailored, navy suit. A blue and red striped necktie hung loosely from her elegant throat. Raine couldn't tell if his heart skipped a beat, or it just felt like that because it was racing so fast.

"You look like a lawyer too," she said to him. "Can you explain to Madam Clerk that I don't need to file a working copy for the judge if I've already filed a copy electronically?"

Raine wasn't sure he could breathe at that moment, let alone speak. But he gathered his wits and nodded around the vision of Aphrodite he found before him at the clerk he had known for years.

"Uh, you don't technically have to," Raine agreed, "but it makes the clerks' lives easier if you do. We all know the local rules, but you know how judges are. They think they know everything. They'll ask the clerk where the paper working copy is, and they won't take kindly to a clerk citing the court rules to them, even if the clerk is right."

The beautiful stranger raised a hand to her face and rubbed her chin. Her nails were short and painted the same candy apple red as her lips. "What did you say your name was?"

"I didn't," Raine replied, "but it's Dan. Dan Raine." He extended a hand and hid his delight when she shook it. A strong, firm grasp. Of course.

"Sawyer. Sawyer Mount." She introduced herself. "I'm new in town. Just moved here from California. I made sure to study all of the local rules, but I guess you can't learn the local customs until you get here, huh?"

"I guess not," Raine agreed. He nodded at the papers in her hand. "Would you like me to show you where the courthouse copier is? It's right by the coffee shop. I could buy you a cup."

Sawyer Mount's lips parted slowly into a dazzling smile. Her teeth were as white as her eyes were blue. "You move fast, Dan Raine. I like that."

And Raine liked that she liked that.

A few minutes later, Sawyer knew where she could make that extra copy of her pleading for ten cents a page, and Raine was paying for a tall cherry mocha for her and a tall Americano for himself. They found a seat at a table near the door and commenced the small talk.

"So, where in California are you from?" Raine opened. "And what brought you to Seattle?"

"Do you know Bakersfield?" Sawyer asked. "Then you know why I came to Seattle."

Raine didn't know that much about Bakersfield, California. His expression likely betrayed his ignorance.

"That's not fair, actually." Sawyer waved away her own words. "I'm not even from Bakersfield. I'm from a town about fifty miles north of it. I wish I were from Bakersfield."

"Okay," Raine said. "So, not a lot of lawyering opportunities there?"

"Not a lot of anything there," Sawyer answered. "I'm not the sort of person who blends in very well with people who aren't like me."

Raine had noticed that.

"And it turned out no one there was like me," Sawyer continued, "so I left. First, to San Francisco for law school. Then San Jose for my first job. Then here."

"You didn't like those places either?" Raine asked.

"Actually, I liked them fine," Sawyer answered. "Especially San Francisco. But I couldn't find a job there doing what I wanted, and San Jose was just too far away and too expensive. I wanted someplace a little smaller. A little less incessantly warm and sunny."

"Seattle has never been accused of being incessantly sunny," Raine confirmed.

"Rain City." Sawyer nodded. "I heard that nickname once, and I immediately knew where I was moving to. I just needed to wrap up my cases first. I couldn't leave my clients in the lurch."

"Couldn't you hand them off to someone else in your firm?" Raine asked. "Or were you solo, like me?"

Sawyer glanced down at Raine's left hand. "You're solo, huh?" She smiled and tapped the same ringless finger on her own left hand. "Me too. But no, I was a public defender. There were plenty of other lawyers in my office, but you can't just hand off a criminal defense case like that, especially not the case I was doing. I had relationships with those people. I was the only thing standing between them and prison."

"Sounds like they were right to," Raine observed.

Sawyer took a moment, then laughed. "Don't get too intense, Dan. It was a job, not necessarily a calling. But if I have a job to do, I'm going to do it right. I wrapped up my last case—an acquittal after a three-week jury trial, thank you very much—and hopped on the I-5 north."

"Just I-5," Raine corrected her. "Everyone will know you're from California if you say 'the I-5'."

Sawyer frowned. "Is that a bad thing?"

"That people know you're from California?" Raine clarified. He shrugged. "People from here don't always trust people who aren't from here. You'll need people to trust you if you want jurors to give you 'not guilty' verdicts too."

Sawyer smiled. "I do want that." Then she looked down at herself. "My appearance might give it away too. I'm not wearing ten shades of black and a frown."

Raine took a moment to appreciate that fact. "No," he agreed. "No, you are not."

Sawyer's eyes glimmered at the compliment. "What about you, Mr. Raine? Do you do criminal defense too?"

"Not if I can avoid it." Raine leaned back in his chair, which only made him realize he had been leaning ever closer to Sawyer as she spoke.

"You don't like helping people?" Sawyer challenged. "Criminals, even?"

"I don't like tilting at windmills," Raine answered. "And I don't like hounding clients to pay me. That's a rough way to make a living."

"Hm." Sawyer nodded slightly and took a sip of her coffee. "I guess not everyone likes it rough."

Raine was struck speechless, a rare condition for a lawyer.

Sawyer took a long, deep swig of her coffee and slammed the empty cup on the table. "I'll tell you what, Daniel Raine, I need to get my working copies to the judge, and you need to get whatever you came here to file filed. Give me your phone, and I'll give you my number. Let's continue this conversation over stronger drinks and an expensive dinner."

Raine could hardly argue with any of that. Especially the reminder that he needed to file Adam's lawsuit before his father got wind of it. That wasn't the most important take-away, but it was the most urgent. He handed over his phone in a way that he hoped didn't seem too rushed and eager, then gladly accepted it back. He glanced down and saw that she had even added her name to his contacts. "Sawyer". They were already on a first-name basis.

"See you around, Dan," she said as she turned toward the hallway to the copier. "Don't leave a girl waiting."

*Excellent advice*, Raine thought as he watched Sawyer Mount walk away. After a moment, he realized it also applied to the court clerk, and he hurried back downstairs to file his lawsuit.

## 5
---

R aine had also not left the courier waiting. As soon as the lawsuit was filed, Raine generated a case schedule, noted the first preliminary hearing, and bundled all of the documents into a packet to be served on Bill Harper that same afternoon. Raine made a phone call to Adam to warn him, then sat back and waited for the explosion his conversations with Adam led him to believe would occur.

Instead, nothing happened. Bill Harper didn't show up on his doorstep to challenge him to a fistfight, and no responsive pleadings were filed and served on him either. As the first hearing approached, Raine almost felt as if he had never filed the case.

Adam wasn't returning his calls either. Maybe the very threat of the lawsuit had brought the Harpers to the table to reach some sort of agreement. If so, Raine was glad he'd made sure to get paid in advance of what little work he had already done. But until he heard differently from his client, he had to assume the litigation was going forward.

Raine had scheduled the preliminary hearing for a Monday, in no small part because Monday morning was the worst time to have to do anything, and he wanted to pile the misery on his opponent. It also protected the hearing from any last-minute filings. From the standpoint of the court rules, the last minute before a Monday morning hearing was 5:00 the previous Friday. If Harper and his lawyer did file something "last minute", Raine would still have the entire weekend to decide how to respond.

Raine made a trip to the courthouse that Friday afternoon. In theory, he should have been able to see any new filings on the court's website. In practice, the clerks weren't going to upload anything filed late on a Friday afternoon. If Raine wanted to be sure nothing had been filed, he needed to be in the clerk's office in person when the courthouse closed for the week. He checked the court file one last time at 4:00, then sat in the lobby and waited to see if anyone came in on a rainy Friday afternoon. No one did, and Raine walked back to the courthouse certain of, and surprised by, the fact that Bill Harper had in no way responded to the lawsuit brought against him by his own son.

The rain had grown heavier while he was inside. Raine lowered his face against the diagonally falling drops and focused on avoiding the puddles accumulating on the uneven pavement. When he made the last turn onto Washington Street, he raised his gaze again to spy the familiar sight of his office building—and the unfamiliar sight of a man holding an umbrella in the rain.

It wasn't that umbrellas weren't effective against the rain. Of course they were. But they were large and unwieldy. If everyone used one, then there would be no space for anyone to walk down the sidewalk. And once you were inside, they were wet and drippy and annoying to carry around. It was much easier to push back the hood of a raincoat and get on with your business. As a result, the only people who used umbrellas in Seattle were tourists or rich folk whose clothes were too fancy to wear a hooded raincoat over. The sort of folk who didn't care if they left enough space for other people to use the sidewalk.

The man in question appeared to fall into the latter category. He was wearing the fine suit and lavish overcoat of a rich man. He was also standing directly in front of Raine's office and appeared to be examining Raine's car parked directly in front of it.

"Can I help you?" Raine called out as he walked up behind the man.

The man turned around slowly, as if in no hurry despite the rain and Raine's approach. He was tall, with thick black hair and a neatly trimmed beard. His eyes were bright despite the shadow from his umbrella.

"Dan?" the man said. "It is you, isn't it?"

Raine stopped and took a moment to assess the man casing his workplace. His face was familiar, but Raine couldn't quite place him. The thing about being a lawyer was that you met a lot of people over the years, and at least half of them were upset with you. It was good to know who you were dealing with before closing any gaps on the sidewalk.

"Do I know you?" Raine asked. Obviously, he did. Or at least the man knew him. Raine's mind tried to find a name to match the face, but to no avail. It wasn't anyone he'd interacted with recently, Raine was sure enough about that, but the longer ago it had been, the greater the challenge to remember. Not only do memories fade, but faces change.

Although this man looked to take care of himself. He probably hadn't aged noticeably since...

"Law school," the man said. "We went to law school together. Don't you remember me?"

And Raine suddenly did. His stomach dropped. He remembered the man, and he remembered that he never really liked him. Some people were better left in the past.

"Zac Chapman." Raine extracted the name from his memory. "I haven't seen you in—"

"Too long," Chapman finished the sentence. He gestured at the office window, with its "Raine Law Offices" stencil. "I figured that was you."

Raine glanced at the window himself. The office suddenly seemed very small.

"That's me," Raine confirmed. "And that's my car." He nodded at the late model sedan Chapman had been inspecting. "What brings you to my neck of the woods, Zac? Do you need a lawyer?"

Chapman laughed, but humorlessly. "No, Dan. If I needed a lawyer, I don't think I'd be checking out storefront solo practitioners in the International District. Although, you never know. It seems like you've been able to keep yourself afloat."

"You're just out for a walk, then?" Raine questioned.

Chapman smiled at the question, but didn't answer it. "Aren't you going to ask me how I'm doing? What I've been up to since law school?"

"To be honest," Raine answered, "I haven't thought of you much since law school. Probably not at all. Like half our class. Law school was terrible. They make it that way on purpose. I forgot as much about it as I could as fast as I could. I guess that included you." He didn't add, "Sorry."

"I'm doing well, thank you." Chapman answered his own question anyway. "Got in with one of the top firms in the city. Made partner right on schedule. Own a house on Lake Washington and a condo in Palm Springs."

"Good for you," Raine said. "Well, if you're not here to see me, I'm going to go inside my office. This rain isn't letting up."

"I'm not here to consult you," Chapman replied, "but I'm glad I got to see you, Dan."

Raine couldn't quite bring himself to offer the same sentiment. Chapman undoubtedly noticed.

"Say hi to Natalie for me," he added before turning to disappear into the drizzle.

Raine watched after him, having fully recalled why he didn't like Zachary Chapman.

# 6

Another woman Raine knew not to keep waiting was his ex-wife, Natalie. At least not when it was time to pick up or drop off their two boys. Although, Raine had come to accept that was really the only time they interacted anymore anyway. The boys were with him that weekend, so after work, he drove to what had once been their shared home. Now, it was just Natalie's house. And it was still raining.

Raine parked in the driveway and trudged to the front door. At least there was an overhang, so he could pull his hood back. He rang the bell and waited until he heard the sound of his boys yelling at each other to grab their bags, and the sound of Natalie unlocking the door.

"Hey, Dan," she said without really looking at him. "The boys are almost ready. They lost track of time playing some new video game."

"No problem," Raine replied. And it wasn't. A few minutes here and there weren't going to change how his boys felt about him. Getting angry about those few minutes would.

The bigger problem was the awkward silence while two people who used to love each other stood facing each other with nothing more to say to each other.

The danger was that one of them would blurt something out just to fill the awkward silence. That night, it was Raine who did it. When it came to Natalie, it was usually Raine who did it. She seemed far better able to tolerate the awkwardness their love had withered into.

"I saw Zac Chapman today," Raine heard himself say, somehow detached by the knowledge that he shouldn't say it.

Natalie's stoic expression livened up. "Zac Chapman?" She laughed lightly. "I'd forgotten all about him."

"He said to say hi," Raine added. There was something about the engagement in her voice that made him want to keep it alive.

"He did?" Natalie laughed again and tucked a lock of hair behind her ear. "Wow."

The unspoken truth was that Chapman had also been interested in Natalie back in the day. It hadn't been a competition in the truest sense of that word. Raine had already been dating Natalie when Chapman first started hanging out with their friend group. It was that Chapman didn't seem to care. He made his affections and intentions well known. Natalie seemed to enjoy the attention but nothing more. And Raine was confident enough in their relationship, and himself, not to make too big a deal out of it. But it had always bothered him. It still did. Just like Natalie had always sort of liked it. And apparently still did.

There was a reason Raine had cut off contact with Chapman after they stopped having classes together.

"Well, say hi to him from me, then," Natalie said after a moment.

"I doubt I'll see him again," Raine answered. "I just ran into him outside my office."

"Oh," Natalie replied. Then, "That reminds me. I haven't seen the child support money yet for this month. If you need a little more time to pull it together, I understand, but I do use that money to pay for things the boys need."

"What?" Raine was shocked. He pulled his phone out of his pocket to open his banking app. "No. I paid it. I'm sure."

"Dan, really, it's okay," Natalie assured him. "Just try to get it to me by the fifteenth if you can. If you need some extra time next month, that's okay too. I just need to know how to budget."

"No, no," Raine insisted, tapping his phone frantically to find the transaction. "I paid it. I'm sure I did. Where is it?" Then he realized what he had likely done. He opened a different account in the same app and confirmed. "Oh, shit. I see what I did. I accidentally tried to send it from my business account instead of my personal account. But I had just given myself my monthly draw, so there wasn't anything in there."

"You don't have to explain," Natalie assured him. "Just get it to me whenever you can."

"I can do it right now," Raine grumbled. He started tapping at his phone again, but then his boys came tumbling out of the house.

"Dad," his youngest son, Jordan, called out. He was in eighth grade. Sometimes he seemed older. Sometimes younger. "Where are we going for dinner? Can we go to Pasta Kingdom? Please?"

"No," Jason, his older brother, called out as he traversed the doorway, his eyes momentarily—and only momentarily—off the phone in his hand. "I hate Pasta Kingdom."

"Have fun tonight, Dan." Natalie stepped back to close the door.

"I'll send the money as soon as I get a minute," Dan promised. "Once we're seated and waiting on the spaghetti Bolognese."

"Yes! We're going to Pasta Kingdom!" Jordan shouted.

"Dad!" Jason whined. Then he just huffed, buried his face in his phone again, and stomped toward the car.

"Whatever you say, Dan," Natalie replied. "It's fine."

She started to shut the front door when something dawned on Raine.

"Why did my mentioning Zac Chapman remind you that I hadn't paid the child support yet?"

Natalie didn't answer the question. She just cocked her head and smiled gently at him. "It's fine," she repeated, and closed the door.

## 7

By the end of the weekend, Raine had almost managed to forget about Zac Chapman. Until he walked into court Monday morning and saw Chapman seated at the defendant's table, next to a large man Raine knew had to be Bill Harper. Seated in the gallery directly behind Bill Harper was a middle-aged couple dressed in oppressively conservative business suits. Judging by the family resemblance among the Harper men, Raine deduced the man was Adam's brother, Mark; that would make the woman Mark's wife, whose name Raine had already forgotten.

"Raine," Chapman called out, his arm swung confidently over the back of his chair. He had been watching the door, waiting for Raine's arrival. "So good to see you again. This is going to be fun."

Raine doubted that. Chapman and the elder Harper looked like formidable foes. Both dressed to impress and larger than life. Bill Harper was seated, but Raine could tell he was tall, with a bald head, thick neck, and meaty hands. Chapman was tall too, but in an athletic way, a cut physique beneath his expensive suit.

Raine was wearing his own best suit and was an imposing enough character in his own right. But his client was missing in action.

"Where's little Adam?" Chapman asked with a grin. "Did you lose him at the playground?"

"I'm sure the younger Mr. Harper will be here any moment," Raine replied evenly. He set his briefcase onto the plaintiff's table and began extracting his materials. The case file, his copy of the court rules, a yellow legal pad. The weapons of the trial attorney. "Strange you didn't mention you had been retained on this case when we ran into each other last Friday."

"I thought it was strange you didn't figure it out immediately," Chapman responded. "I hadn't seen you for two decades, and then I suddenly show up outside your office after you file a lawsuit against one of Seattle's richest developers. You remember the passion I always had for construction law, right?"

"I barely remembered your name," Raine replied without looking at him.

Chapman paused. "Did you say hi to Natalie for me?"

Raine knew to take a moment before replying to that goad. Fortunately, after that moment, Adam Harper rushed into the courtroom.

"I'm here," he announced, quite unnecessarily. Then he spied the couple seated behind his father. "Mark. Sarah." He sneered at his brother and sister-in-law. "I guess I shouldn't be surprised you'd show up to support Dad."

Mark didn't say anything in response. Sarah nudged him, but rather than reply to his brother, he looked to his father. His father wasn't looking at him.

Adam finished his walk to the plaintiff's table to join Raine. "I'm sorry I didn't get here any sooner. There is no parking near the courthouse. Did I miss anything?"

"Just some trash-talking," Raine answered, with a sidelong glance at his opposing counsel. "Nothing important."

"Are we ready?" Adam panted. "Are *you* ready?"

Raine was about to offer a confident, if clichéd, "I'm always ready," but before he could, they were interrupted by a weak cough and even weaker, "Excuse me."

Raine turned to see Mark Harper trying to get his attention. Sarah stood behind him, glowering at, well, everyone, it seemed.

"Excuse me, Mr. Raine," Mark repeated. "I was wondering if we could talk to you very briefly before the hearing begins."

Raine looked at the clock on the courtroom wall. "If the judge takes the bench on time, you have two minutes," he said. "What do you want to talk about?"

Adam crossed his arms and matched Sarah's glower, directing it exclusively at his brother.

"Yes. Excellent. Thank you." Mark wrung his hands slowly. "It's just that I want you to know, and Adam as well, I suppose, since he's insisting on standing here while we talk."

"He's my client." Raine was surprised he needed to explain. "I won't be keeping secrets from my client."

"Yes. Quite right. Of course not," Mark agreed with a staccato of nods. "I just wanted you to know that we are really hoping to not end up in the middle of this litigation. I do not want to be called to testify against my father or my brother. I'm hopeful that you and your colleague across the aisle will be able to come to some mutually beneficial settlement that will obviate the need for me or Sarah to testify."

Raine twisted his mouth into a thoughtful frown. He looked first to Adam Harper. Then to Bill Harper. Then finally to Zac Chapman. Then he returned his gaze to Mark Harper. "I don't believe a settlement is likely in this case, Mr. Harper. You should prepare yourself to give testimony. Whether it's against your father or against your brother will be up to you. I just hope it's the truth."

Sarah shoved her husband's shoulder from behind. "See? I told you it was a waste of time. Stupid idea."

Mark didn't look like he was necessarily going to say anything back to his wife, but he didn't get the chance anyway.

The bailiff stood up and bellowed, "The King County Superior Court is now in session! The Honorable Jacqueline Malloy presiding!"

Judge Malloy emerged from her chambers and took her perch atop the bench above the litigants. "You may be seated," she directed.

Malloy was in either her late fifties or early sixties. She had been a judge long enough to be good at it, but not so long to have gotten bad at it again. They could have drawn several worse judges. She was usually the smartest person in the room but professional enough not to need everyone to acknowledge it. Gray hair swept back from soft wrinkles and a pair of glasses that took up half of her face. A face that wasn't smiling. She was ready to get down to business. That was fine with Raine.

"Are the parties ready on the matter of *Harper versus Harper*?" the judge asked.

Raine stood up to address the Court. "Plaintiff Adam Harper is ready, Your Honor." Then, for the record, and just in case the judge didn't remember the handful of times he'd appeared before her over what was fast becoming too many years as a lawyer. "Attorney Daniel Raine appearing on behalf of the plaintiff."

Chapman was on his feet before Raine finished his last sentence. "Zachary Chapman of the law firm of D.K.M-Arnold, appearing on behalf of the defendant, William J. Harper. And yes, the defense is more than ready, Your Honor."

Raine was remembering all of the reasons he hadn't liked Chapman even way back in law school, regardless of his interest in Raine's then-girlfriend. He was smarmy and overconfident. Normally that sort of personality was off-putting, but it could find space to thrive in the legal professional.

"Good to see you again, Mr. Chapman," Judge Malloy replied. And before Raine could think she might be playing favorites already, she turned to him and added, "It's nice to see you in my courtroom again as well, Mr. Raine. I am looking forward to presiding over a case involving two competent and experienced counsel."

Adam grabbed Raine's jacket sleeve. "She knows both of you?" he whispered. "I don't like that."

"You don't like that the judge is being fair and evenhand-ed?" Raine whispered back.

"No," Adam confirmed. "I don't want her to be even-handed. I want her to be on our side."

Raine sighed through his nose. "Let me do the talking," he answered, "and she will be, soon enough."

Adam thought for a moment, then let go of Raine's sleeve. He smiled slightly and settled back into his chair.

"Is there a problem, Mr. Raine?" Judge Malloy asked.

"No problem at all, Your Honor," Raine insisted with a practiced smile, even though he knew that the judge knew it was a lie. Chapman knew it too.

"If Mr. Raine needs a moment to calm his client, Your Honor," he offered, "we could take a brief recess. Perhaps the weight of an actual courtroom is giving him second thoughts about pursuing this quixotic claim."

Raine rolled his eyes. Chapman would use a word like "quixotic" unironically.

"We're fine, Your Honor," Raine assured her. "And we're ready to move ahead with this morning's hearing. My client is eager to set the case schedule and select a trial date."

"Trial date?" Chapman scoffed. He pretended to stifle a manufactured laugh. "Let's not get ahead of ourselves, Mr. Raine. The first things we need to schedule are our varied motions to dismiss."

Before Raine could offer a rejoinder, the judge stepped in.

"We will establish the entire case schedule this morning, counsel," she declared. "That will include the selection of a trial date, and a timeline for discovery. It can also include any motions to dismiss or other motions either side feels it appropriate to file." Then, the slightest tilt of her head toward Chapman. "There's no need to grandstand this morning. There's no jury here for you to impress, and I can assure you I won't be impressed by such conduct."

The problem, Raine knew, was that the clients would be impressed. Chapman wasn't trying to sway the judge. He wasn't even trying to psych out Raine, although he would have been happy with that as well. Chapman's audience was Bill Harper. Just as Raine's was Bill Harper's younger son.

"We have several motions we would like to schedule," Chapman persisted. "A motion to dismiss for failure to state claim, a motion for summary judgment, and a motion for a directed verdict."

Judge Malloy lowered her glasses to glance at Chapman over them. "Of course, Mr. Chapman, but would you mind if I ran this hearing? Unless you were planning on running for judge soon?"

He probably was, Raine supposed. He had that sort of ambition—ambition for its own sake.

Chapman just grinned at the question. Then he reached into his briefcase and extracted a stack of papers about two inches thick. "We have already prepared the written motions and supporting briefs for our motions, Your Honor. We understand that the Court will need to reserve all possible dates, but the defendant would urge the Court to schedule our dispositive motions as soon as possible under the court rules. Two weeks from today at the absolute latest."

The judge gestured to her bailiff, who rose and fetched the pleadings from Chapman.

Chapman then provided Raine with his copies of the documents, also required by court rule.

"These motions will be added to the case schedule," Judge Malloy continued as Raine began examining Chapman's motions, "along with standard discovery cut-offs and a trial date. I will not tell the lawyers how to prepare their cases, but I warn both sides that I will not extend the dead-lines for depositions or interrogatories because one side or the other expected to win a motion that would make those deadlines moot."

Raine stood up. "Your Honor, I think it may be in every-one's best interests to schedule these motions out a little further than two weeks. Mr. Chapman wants the Court to find that there is no material issue of fact regarding his client's mental capacity, but I would submit that his client's mental capacity is the central issue of fact in this case, and one that can only properly be determined by a jury after discovery is complete. We will be seeking a mental examina-tion of the defendant—"

"We have already completed one," Chapman inter-rupted, pulling another document from his briefcase.

"One performed by our own expert," Raine continued.

"No objection," Chapman responded. "We'll do it today."

Raine chewed the inside of his cheek for a moment. "The point is, Your Honor, that this is a serious and complicated case that is going to take time to properly investigate and prepare. No one is served by rushing into motions that aren't ripe yet."

"The point is, Your Honor," Chapman countered, "that time is of the essence. There is a multimillion-dollar busi-ness in the balance."

"All the more reason to be careful," Raine submitted.

"All the more reason to end this farce as soon as possi-ble," Chapman implored.

"Okay, that's enough from both of you." Judge Malloy raised her hands. "We are here to establish the case schedule for the motions and trial. We are not here to argue those motions and that trial."

"I want to get this over with as soon as possible too," Adam whispered to Raine.

Raine shook his head. "No, you don't."

"Your Honor." Chapman spoke up again. "Would the Court be willing to hear directly from my client?"

That sent a visible wave of discomfort through the judge. There were a lot of reasons why lawyers represented people in court. One of those reasons, at least for those inside the profession, was to avoid having to hear from the parties themselves. Lawyers were supposed to be dispassionate professionals, able to translate their clients' chaotic thoughts and feelings into coherent legal arguments. Even the worst lawyer was better than hearing from the actual litigant, with all of their fear and anger just looking for a venue to explode in.

"Your client?" Judge Malloy raised an eyebrow. "And why would I do that?"

And why would Chapman offer up his client to speak at the very first hearing? Raine wondered. Generally, it was best to control everything your client said, and to minimize it if at all possible. Raine was expecting to have to fight for every word he extracted from his eventual deposition of Bill Harper, with Harper stonewalling and Chapman objecting after every question.

"This entire case is based on an allegation that my client is mentally unfit to run his business," Chapman explained. "Nothing could be further from the truth. Our first motion is a motion for summary judgment. We will be asking the Court to find that no reasonable jury could possibly find my client to be mentally unfit, and to therefore dismiss the case. There are very important reasons why that hearing needs to occur as soon as possible, and we believe that if Mr. Harper is given the opportunity to explain those reasons to the Court himself, then the Court will see that we are exceedingly likely to prevail on that motion, and will therefore agree to schedule it as soon as legally permissible."

Judge Malloy's mouth twisted into a thoughtful, or perhaps annoyed, knot. After a moment, she nodded down at the plaintiff's table. "Any objection, Mr. Raine?"

"Do I object to my opposing party speaking unchecked in open court, with a court reporter taking down every word, regarding a procedural question that is already adequately addressed by the court rules?" Raine asked facetiously. "No, Your Honor, I have no objection."

He could be smarmy and overconfident too.

Malloy shrugged her black-robed shoulders. "Fine, then. I will hear from the defendant directly as to why I should schedule the defense motion to dismiss sooner rather than later. Whenever you're ready, Mr. Harper."

Bill Harper carefully slid his chair backward and pushed himself to his feet. He was wearing a coat and tie, but in that way men who never wore a coat and tie did. He probably hadn't worn it since the last family wedding he had been forced to attend. He was a builder who built a company. He had wealth, but he was from wages.

"Thank you, Your Honor," he began in a low gravelly voice that betrayed years of cigarettes and bourbon. "I would also like to thank my attorney, Mr. Chapman, for agreeing to ask the Court for permission for me to speak. He advised against it. He explained all of the reasons why it was dangerous for a party to a lawsuit to speak outside of the very controlled settings of a deposition and a trial. However, I explained to him why it was dangerous for me not to speak, and he listened. For that I am grateful, and impressed."

Raine sat at the plaintiff's table, hands folded and eyes fixed on his opponent. Whatever half-contained glee he had been feeling at the prospect of Bill Harper tripping over his tongue in open court was ebbing slowly but steadily into a pool on the floor around his chair.

"As Mr. Chapman pointed out," Bill Harper continued, "and the Court already knows, the primary assertion at the core of this case is that I am no longer mentally capable of running the company I built, literally and figuratively, from the ground up. I am disappointed that my own son would level such a baseless allegation against me, but I also understand that he has a right to his day in court and that there are procedures in place to make sure every case, not just mine, is resolved in as fair and as timely a fashion as possible, given all of the other cases that are filed every day here in this very courthouse."

Judge Malloy's shoulders were no longer shrugging. They were squared at the man speaking to her, and she leaned forward as she listened, intently.

"But I would like the Court to understand, Your Honor," Bill Harper continued, "that there are certain aspects to my case which may differ from at least some of the others making their way through the King County court system. Prime among these is the impact this litigation is already having, and will continue to have, on the very business being fought over. Harper Development is in the middle of its largest project ever, the construction of what will be Seattle's tallest residential condominium tower. There are workers who need to be paid, contractors who need to be hired, permits to be pulled, and banks to be paid. None of that can happen when ownership of the company is in doubt.

"It isn't fair to the workers to not get paid because no one knows who is authorized to sign the checks. It isn't fair to the subcontractors to lose out on a project that could pay their employees for six months because no one knows who is authorized to sign the contract. It isn't fair to the investors in this project that the next stage in construction might not be able to proceed because no one knows who is authorized to apply for the next set of permits from the city. I would say it's not fair to the banks either, but they're banks. They'll get their money one way or another."

Judge Malloy laughed lightly, and Raine knew he was in big trouble.

"I'm not asking the Court to dismiss the case today," Bill Harper concluded, "but I am asking the Court to consider that request at the earliest opportunity under the law. I am confident that I am mentally fit to run my own company. I hope my words and comport here today have made the Court think that might also be the case. And if the Court agrees that there is no true issue as to my mental capability, then the sooner we can reach that decision, the sooner this project can get back on track, and the sooner everyone can get back to their job."

Chapman threw another glance over at them, and Adam in particular. They both knew there was one person who wouldn't be going back to his job at Harper Development if his gambit to take over the company failed.

"Thank you for listening to me, Your Honor." Then Bill Harper sat down again.

Judge Malloy rubbed her chin for several very long moments, then turned again to the plaintiff's table. "I'm going to schedule the defendant's motion to dismiss in two weeks, Mr. Raine."

Raine knew she was going to say that. And he was pretty sure what she was going to say after that hearing as well.

———

RAINE SHOOK his head as he paced outside on the courthouse steps with his client after the hearing. "We are," he said, "to use the Latin, fucked."

Adam frowned at him. "I didn't hire you to give up."

"Actually, I'm not sure why you hired me." Raine stopped pacing and locked eyes with his client. He pointed at the courthouse behind him. "Did you hear your father just now? He was more eloquent than anyone else who spoke at that hearing, including the judge. She is probably already preparing the order to dismiss the case."

"What about that expert you said was going to examine him?" Adam suggested.

"Do you think he's going to say your old man has lost it?" Raine questioned. "Because he doesn't seem like he's lost it."

"Isn't that what we pay the expert for?" Adam asked. "He says whatever we tell him to say, right?"

Raine cocked his head at his client. "You think we hire a Ph.D. in psychology to examine your dad, and then he just says whatever we tell him to say because we pay him off?"

"Is that not how it works?" Adam asked.

"That is not how it works," Raine answered. "We pay them for their time, and yeah, if they want to get hired again, maybe they decide the close calls in our favor. But this isn't close. No licensed psychologist is going to destroy their professional credibility by claiming that someone who is very obviously not senile is senile. Their reputation would never survive that."

Adam looked down and thought for several seconds. He looked up again and met Raine's frustrated gaze. "So what's going to happen in two weeks?"

"Absent some sudden and significant change in circumstances," Raine declared, "the case is going to get dismissed, and you're going to be out on the street."

———————

## 8

Raine stormed back to his office, unsure what he could do to salvage the case. It was possible Old Man Harper had good days and bad, times when he was more lucid than others. Maybe that was as good as it got for him—but it was pretty damn good. There was still a chance he would be far less coherent at the hearing two weeks later, but Raine couldn't count on that. He didn't expect it either.

He spent the day updating his billing on the case. He wasn't going to lose money on it, but he wasn't going to make much either. The best thing, both for the case and for his bank account, was to press ahead, do the mental examinations, write the briefs, conduct the hearing, and bill Adam Harper for every minute of it until Judge Malloy announced, "Case dismissed."

By the time five o'clock rolled around, Raine was still billing hours, and Laura was headed out the door. Raine noted the sound of the front door closing and called out a belated, "Have a good night!"

He hardly expected a reply, so his heart jumped when Rebecca Sommers called back, "We'll see!"

"Holy sh—!" Raine grabbed at his chest. Sommers was in his office doorway, grinning ear to ear. "You scared me to death."

"Half to death, maybe." Sommers nodded disapprovingly at him. "I mean, you do look kind of half dead right now. Tough day in court?"

"You knew I had court today?" Raine found himself surprised by her attention to his details. He supposed he shouldn't be anymore.

"I pay attention," she answered. "And I remember things."

"Good habits," Raine admired.

"So I thought I'd stop by at the end of the day and see if you wanted to grab a drink," Sommers continued. "If your day went well, we could celebrate. If not, we could commiserate."

"Commiserate." Raine answered the underlying question. "Definitely commiserate."

"That's too bad," Sommers answered.

Raine shrugged. "The good news is I'll be a lot less busy after the case gets dismissed in two weeks."

"Dismissed?" Sommers asked. "Why?"

"Because Bill Harper is the opposite of mentally unfit." Raine answered both questions at once. "He spoke in court, and quite eloquently I must admit. Unless he loses his mind between now and the hearing, I don't see how the judge can say there's any basis for the case to go forward."

"What about some sort of mental examination?" Sommers suggested.

"He already did one," Raine answered, "and he's agreed to do another one with our expert before the hearing."

"Do you have an expert?"

"Not yet," Raine admitted, "but I don't think it will matter anyway. From what I heard today, there's not a psychologist in town who would find him mentally unfit."

Sommers nodded as she considered the information. "I think you're going to want to talk to Meredith sooner rather than later."

"Who's Meredith?" Raine asked.

"A friend of a friend," Sommers answered. "She owns an HVAC company. She says Bill Harper terminated her contract on that new tower they're building. He came to her office personally to tell her. If he's showing any signs of being crazy, she would know."

"You're always a step ahead of me." Raine sighed.

"What about dinner tomorrow night?" Sommers suggested. "Someplace fancy. We could expense it, right?"

Raine laughed slightly. "An expensive dinner tomorrow night isn't going to work for me. For one thing, I don't have a fancy expense account I use for tax write-offs. I'm just trying to earn enough money to have to pay taxes in the first place."

Sommers smiled, but awkwardly. She obviously had a fancy expense account. "So that's the one thing why you can't meet Meredith tomorrow night. What's the other thing?"

Raine grinned, the first genuine smile since Sommers had darkened his door. "I have a date."

## 9

One of the advantages of going on a date with someone new to town was the likelihood that they hadn't been to all of the best date spots yet. Raine could impress Sawyer with even the most tired first-date venues. On the other hand, Sawyer didn't seem like the type of person who was easily impressed. Not by a choice of restaurant, anyway. So Raine decided to take a risk and impress her with himself. And the city's best cocktails.

Sawyer glanced around the trenchlike confines of Post Alley and at the unmarked door tucked halfway between Stewart and Virginia Streets. "No windows with a view of the water, I'm guessing," she commented.

"I don't think this place has any windows at all," Raine replied. "But if you're looking for the city's best old-fashioned, this is where you'll find it."

"I'm more of a Negroni girl," Sawyer replied. She was dressed similarly to the first time Raine had seen her. An androgynous mix of men's jacket, sleeves rolled, and women's pants, a chunky wristwatch, no earrings, and red high heels that made her almost equal to Raine's six feet three inches.

There was a joke in there about Sawyer being a "California girl", but Raine avoided it, proud of the decision. "You can be any kind of girl you want in here," he said instead. Much better. Mysterious. Inviting.

Sawyer cocked her head at Raine and laughed. "That's a pretty good line. You speak for a living or something?"

"Yeah, something like that." Raine returned the laugh. Then he knocked on the door to the speakeasy. "Let's drink and tell war stories."

"A perfect first date," Sawyer agreed.

---

"SO THEN I turned back to the jury and said, 'I rest my case!'" Sawyer slammed her hand on the table as she finished her story.

Raine burst out laughing. "That is amazing. Did you win?"

"Oh, no." Sawyer laughed. "They convicted in, like, ten minutes. But I won the appeal, and now that prosecutor is doing tax law or some boring shit in Riverside."

"Serves him right." Raine raised his glass to her.

Sawyer clinked hers to his and slammed back the remainder of what was probably her third drink, but maybe her fourth. Raine had lost count as his own drink count increased.

"We should probably eat something." He reached for the coaster with the QR code for the menu. Sawyer followed suit.

"Oh dear," Raine said after perusing the bar's limited offerings.

"Agreed," Sawyer replied. "There's not much in the way of food. Could you fill up on just olives and peanuts?"

"I like olives," Raine answered, "but not that many. We're going to need to go someplace else for dinner, I think. Sorry about that."

"Don't be sorry," Sawyer assured him. "The drinks were top tier. Now we can find food to match. Let's settle up and head out."

Raine tried to pay, but Sawyer insisted on splitting the check. Then she informed him that she was more than willing to let him pay for dinner, since that was going to be considerably more expensive.

"I know a place," Sawyer expounded as they stepped out of the speakeasy. Night had descended while they were inside. The alley was illuminated by a few infrequent street-lamps and the glow from the nearby road. "Excellent first-date vibes."

"Oh, really?" Raine felt both surprised and a little disap-pointed that Sawyer might already have been on some dates since her arrival in town. But he could hardly expect a woman as head turning as her to not have had multiple options for company and dinner. He was just glad she had chosen to be with him tonight. And he could be the type of companion she'd want to see again. "What's the name of it? I might have been there."

He had options too. No reason not to suggest that. Even if he hadn't actually exercised any of those options since the divorce.

Sawyer narrowed her eyes in concentration, then nodded. "I have no idea. But I think it was that way."

They had reached Stewart Street, and Sawyer pointed up the hill, away from the water. Toward most of downtown Seattle.

"So, not on the waterfront," Raine commented. "That narrows it down only slightly. Do you remember anything else about it? Was it a steak house? Or seafood?"

"Yes, steak," Sawyer answered. "And also seafood. Plus other stuff, I'm pretty sure."

"That's not terribly helpful," Raine pointed out.

Sawyer stood up straight and placed her fists on her hips. "Would you like to end our evening together, Mr. Raine? Is that what you want?"

She was definitely the same height as him in those heels. Her blue eyes sparkled from the lights behind Raine. "That is the exact opposite of what I want, Ms. Mount." He gestured up the hill. "Let's go find your steak and seafood and other stuff restaurant. I'm sure we can do it if we work together."

Sawyer smiled at him. "You're a smart man, Daniel Raine. I'm looking forward to seeing how well we work together."

Raine was very much looking forward to that too. But they should probably eat first.

Sawyer slipped her arm through his, and they made their way toward Second Avenue. It actually made it more difficult to walk, but Raine wasn't about to complain. The fresh air was clearing some of the alcohol from his mind, and he felt reasonably sure they weren't going to fall onto the sidewalk. He expected the restaurant was probably on Fifth or Sixth Avenue. There were places to eat before then, but they weren't the sort of places with "first-date vibes".

He tried asking a few more questions to get some information about this restaurant, but Sawyer was of little help. He wondered if it was intentional. A sort of test, perhaps. He decided to play it cool, stop asking questions, and get them to an area where even if they never found Sawyer's restaurant, they could find someplace good to eat. Their quest was going to have an expiration time. Eventually they would get hungry enough to eat at the nearest place and save the mystery restaurant for another night. And Raine realized that was the better plan anyway. A built-in second date.

But when they reached Fourth Avenue, his attention was diverted to the half-finished skyscraper across the street.

"Hey, look at that." Raine pointed at the building. "That's Harper Tower, the condo tower my latest client is trying to take away from his dad. It's the case I was filing when I ran into you at the courthouse."

Sawyer nodded. "Are you going to win?"

"Oh, fuck no." Raine laughed. "His old man came in and gave a speech to rival the Gettysburg Address. The motion to dismiss is scheduled in two weeks. I have no hope of winning."

"No hope?" Sawyer asked. "Well, not with that attitude, I guess."

*Oops.* Raine remembered that while honesty and candor were attractive qualities, so was confidence.

"There's always hope when J. Daniel Raine is on the case," he corrected. "But it's going to take something pretty unexpected to pull victory from the jaws of dismissal."

Sawyer took a moment. "What's the *J* stand for?"

Raine sighed. He shouldn't have mentioned that first initial. But honesty and candor. "Jack. But I'd rather not talk about it."

"Because Jack Daniel's?" Sawyer asked. "Pfft. I'm a woman named Sawyer. My dad wanted his kid to be a woodworker. That was one of the main reasons I went to law school instead."

"Let's talk about dads giving bad names sometime," Raine suggested. "But right now, you want to go take a look at the building? It's pretty nice so far. Maybe I can get you a deal on a condo when it's finished."

"Now I really want you to win your motion," Sawyer answered. "No way your guy gives you a deal if you let his case get dismissed."

"Good point." Raine pulled her toward the Harper Development site. "Now I have even more reason to win."

"Except you're not going to, I hear," Sawyer reminded him.

"Nonsense!" Raine smiled at her. "Where did you hear such a thing?"

"Some rando I met at the courthouse," Sawyer answered with her own grin, her red lips glistening in the streetlights. "But I didn't believe him."

"Yeah, never trust anyone you meet at a courthouse," Raine agreed. "They're all criminals or lawyers."

It was only a few blocks to the construction site. Two large signs hung on the fencing surrounding the block. The larger one announced "ANOTHER WORLD CLASS HARPER DEVELOPMENT PROJECT", while the one on the locked gate warned "DO NOT ENTER – AUTHORIZED PERSONNEL ONLY".

"I guess we're not getting any closer," Sawyer observed. She pulled off a shoe and rubbed her foot. "I love being taller than everyone, but these things are not made for long walks on pavement."

Raine had not taken that into account when suggesting they go so far out of their way. "Oh, sorry about that."

"No worries." Sawyer pulled her shoe back on. "I'm a big girl. I can handle a little pain."

Raine wasn't sure how to respond to that.

Before he could think of anything, Sawyer put her hands to her face and screamed, "Oh my God!"

Raine looked up, down, and all around, but didn't see anything obviously worthy of that reaction.

Sawyer pointed across the street. "That's it! That's the restaurant I was telling you about!"

Raine peered across the street. "Delmonico's," he read the sign over the door. "Oh yeah. I've been there. You're right. Good date vibes."

The next sound Raine expected to hear was Sawyer agreeing with him, or perhaps a car horn from her jumping into traffic to cross the street.

Instead, it was a sound both unnatural and unmistakable. Unnatural, because human beings weren't naturally supposed to fall more than the height of a tree, rather than a hundred feet from a steel deck, and then onto packed earth, rather than a plaza of rock-hard cement. Unmistakable, because that was exactly the sound that exploded behind them inside the construction site. It reminded Raine of a watermelon being smashed—if the watermelon were two hundred pounds and full of bones.

"Holy shit!" Sawyer spun around to look up at the half-finished office tower. "Was that what I think it was?"

Raine nodded, hoping they were wrong but knowing they were right.

Sawyer dashed to the gate and tried to open it, but the lock and chain were secure. A moment later, those high heels were on the ground. A moment after that, Sawyer was over the gate.

Raine took a beat to see if anyone was watching—not that it really mattered, but they were about to trespass—then pulled himself over the gate after his date.

There were no lamps on inside the worksite, so what light there was fell unevenly through the slats of the perimeter fencing. Sawyer was already running into the darkness at the center of the site. Raine sprinted after her. He pulled up right behind where she had come to a stop.

On the pavement, right in front of what would be the main entrance to the unfinished structure, were the crumpled remains of the person who had fallen to his very obvious death. There was no chance he was alive. His body was crushed, and his blood had spattered a radius of several yards. His limbs lay at unnatural angles, but his face, contorted as it was, was turned toward the sky and recognizable.

"I wonder who he was," Sawyer said.

Raine didn't wonder. He knew. "Bill Harper."

## 10

It wasn't the brightness of the police lights that was the most bothersome. It wasn't the alternating blue and red colors. It was the fact they flashed in a pattern that repeated every nine seconds, and once Raine noticed it, he couldn't stop anticipating the start of the next never-ending cycle. They were seated on the curb just outside the gate they had climbed over, surrounded by patrol cars and their throbbing lights.

"I hope they let us go soon." He rubbed the bridge of his nose, pressing his eyes closed against the red and blue strobe.

"They will," Sawyer answered. "It's not a murder scene, and we're not suspects. Now that they have our written statements, the sergeant is just waiting for the detective to give the okay to let us go."

"Is that how it works in California?" Raine asked, opening his eyes again to squint against the patrol cars' onslaught.

Sawyer shrugged. "I'm guessing a bit," she admitted. "I

know what happens to the defendants because they hire me. The witnesses, they're on their own. But that seems to be the standard practice here too, at least according to the police reports I've seen so far."

Raine grunted and nodded slightly, hopeful but not confident they would be leaving anytime in the next hour.

"At least we'll always remember our first date," Sawyer offered with a broad grin.

Raine had to smile back. Especially since "first" and "remember" suggested there would be more. He nodded across the street. "Let's go to Delmonico's next. We can get reservations and walk straight in before any bodies fall from the sky."

"Aw, pssh." Sawyer waved the worry away. "What are the odds of this happening again?"

"Don't ask," Raine warned.

"I'm not that bad of luck," Sawyer insisted. "I promise. One, maybe two dead bodies. That's my limit."

"So we have one more," Raine observed.

"I said maybe," Sawyer pointed out.

"Mr. Raine. Ms. Mount." They looked up at the man who was suddenly standing over them. "I'm Detective Michael Kavendish. Do you have a moment for a few more questions before we let you go home?"

Kavendish was in his late fifties and looked every year of it. A puffy face sat atop a thick neck and neglected body. His frame wasn't overweight so much as under-cared-for. Years of putting the job before himself. Raine guessed he was divorced, with a couple of kids he didn't see as much as he should. But then again, so was he.

"Do we have a choice?" Sawyer asked sharply.

Kavendish shrugged. "I can't make you talk to me, but

I'm curious why you wouldn't want to. You aren't suspects. At least not as of right now. Is there something else I should know?"

Raine jabbed a thumb at her. "She's a criminal defense attorney."

"Ah." Kavendish nodded. "The natural enemy of the police officer."

"The natural predator," Sawyer responded. "I tell all of my clients never to talk to the cops. Why shouldn't I follow my own advice?"

Kavendish shrugged again. Raine suspected he shrugged a lot. "That's fine with me. I'm just trying to make sure I don't miss anything. A man is dead, and it's my job to determine what happened."

"He fell nineteen stories onto cement," Sawyer said. "Seems pretty open and shut. Can we go now?" She grabbed Raine's arm. "We're on our first date."

"Hell of a first date." Kavendish frowned slightly.

"Yeah, not exactly what we had planned," Raine admitted.

"Well, I just have a couple of things I wanted to clarify before I let you good folks get back to your date."

"The date is kind of over," Sawyer said.

"Is it?" Raine frowned.

Sawyer nodded. "Yeah. Dead guy smashed on the pavement kind of killed the vibe. Let's reschedule."

Raine could hardly argue regarding the vibe. And he was grateful for the reschedule.

Sawyer stood up. "Look, I gave a written statement to your sergeant already, wherein I unwisely admitted to trespassing. I'd like to think you won't charge me, given the circumstances, but again, you're a cop, so I can't really trust you to do the right thing. So before I say anything further incriminating, I'm going to Uber home. I haven't eaten all day, I lost my buzz hours ago, and I just want to go to sleep."

She didn't wait for permission. Kavendish didn't bother giving it. As she started to walk away, though, she turned back to Raine, raised her hand to her ear like a phone, and mouthed, "Call me."

Raine was definitely going to do that.

"I like her," Kavendish remarked at Sawyer's retreating figure.

Raine looked after her as well. "Yeah, me too."

After a moment, Kavendish brought the conversation back to the death of Bill Harper. "So you and your companion were just walking along when you heard the victim fall to his death?"

"That's correct," Raine confirmed.

"And you don't have any connection to the victim, is that right?" Kavendish asked.

Raine took a moment. It was a crime to lie to a police officer. They probably wouldn't be charged with trespassing. They had a pretty good reason to hop that fence. But he might well get charged with obstructing the investigation after the fact with no good reason.

"Well, actually," he replied slowly, "I was kind of suing him."

One of Kavendish's unkempt eyebrows shot up. "You were suing William Harper?"

"Well, I wasn't," Raine clarified. "His son was. But I'm his son's lawyer."

"The dead man's son hired you to sue him?" Both of Kavendish's eyebrows were raised.

"Correct," Raine confirmed.

Kavendish thought for a moment. "Were you winning?"

Raine again recalled that lying to a police officer was a crime. "No. We were almost certainly going to lose."

"And now he's dead," Kavendish observed.

"He is," Raine agreed.

Kavendish chewed the inside of his cheek for a few moments. "Don't you think that's a little suspicious?"

Raine thought for a moment. "Actually, yes. I think it's very suspicious."

## 11

"That does seem suspicious," Sommers agreed the next day.

They were sitting in the conference room in Raine's office, awaiting their guest. The afternoon sun shone through the windows, and Laura had brewed a fresh pot of coffee.

"That's why I need to talk to him," Raine said. "And that's why I need you here. This isn't a conversation to have without witnesses."

"And you trust my instincts when it comes to judging people, right?" Sommers added.

Raine took a moment. "Sure," he agreed. "Let's say it's that too."

Sommers frowned at him, but he knew it was playful. Rebecca Sommers was more than confident enough in her people skills. A friendly jab by Raine wasn't going to make a scratch in that.

"Mr. Harper is here to see you," Laura came in to announce a few minutes later.

"Right on time," Raine noted. He wasn't sure it had any bearing on what they were about to discuss, but at least Adam wasn't wasting their time.

Adam Harper marched into the conference room, a spring in his step and a smile across his face. "Mr. Raine, it's great to see you again. Ms. Sommers," he added with a nod to her.

"You seem to be in a chipper mood," Raine observed.

"You know your dad's dead, right?" Sommers got right to it.

Adam took a moment to reply. If he was shocked by Sommers's statement, it was by the bluntness of it, not its content. "Oh yes. I'm fully aware."

Raine couldn't help but wonder just how fully Adam was aware.

"An amazing coincidence, don't you think?" Raine observed. "We needed something—how did I phrase it?"

"A sudden and significant change in circumstances," Adam repeated what Raine had told them at the end of the court hearing. "This would qualify, right?"

"Are you at all upset that your father is dead?" Sommers asked.

Adam smiled at her, but didn't answer. Instead he looked at the pot of coffee in the center of the table. "Can I get a cup of that?"

"Help yourself." Raine waved a hand at the coffee service. "But answer Rebecca's question. Are you upset your dad died?"

"I mean, sure," Adam allowed as he poured the black liquid into a white mug. "He was my dad. But I'm not heartbroken. We were already on the outs before I filed my lawsuit. And now I win."

"You win?" Raine questioned. "You think this means we win the lawsuit?"

"Doesn't it?" Adam asked, drawing a sip of coffee over the lip of his mug. "It's like a forfeit, right? He's dead. We win."

"He's dead. Our case gets dismissed," Raine returned, with a shake of his head.

"Dismissed?" Adam stopped from taking another drink of his coffee. "Why would it be dismissed? I'm not the one who fell off the nineteenth floor of a half-finished building."

"You're right," Raine agreed.

"You're also very specific," Sommers noted.

"If the other team doesn't play the game, you win by forfeit," Adam repeated his analogy. "Right?"

"It's not a football game," Raine chided. "You were challenging your father's control of the company. Now that he's dead, he doesn't control the company. You can't take something away from someone who doesn't have it."

"Especially if the reason he doesn't have it is that he's dead," Sommers added. Then she reached out to pour herself a cup of coffee as well.

Adam took several moments to consider what he was being told. Finally, he set his mug down a bit too hard on the table. "I thought if Dad died, I would automatically win the lawsuit and own the company."

"You thought wrong," Sommers shot back.

"The lawsuit has been rendered moot by your father's death," Raine expounded. "Our case will be dismissed, and control of the company will pass according to the terms of his will."

The color ran out of Adam's face. "His will? Do we have his will? Did he change it after I filed the lawsuit? Do I still get part of the company?"

There was a reason Raine had scheduled their meeting for the afternoon. There were several reasons, actually, including how late he had been up the night before on what had to be the worst first date in the history of first dates. But another reason was to give him time to track down a copy of Bill Harper's will. Chapman was an ass, but when Raine had called him that morning, he was more than happy to provide Raine with bad news. Raine pulled the will out from the folder that had been sitting to one side and slid it across to Adam.

"He changed it the day after the lawsuit," Raine informed his client. "Instead of an even split, now everything goes to your brother."

"That's outrageous!" Adam slammed a fist on the table, spilling coffee from both his mug and Sommers's. "Mark can't run the company. It'll be bankrupt in a year."

Raine had no reason to believe that was or wasn't true. It didn't matter. "That may be, but it's his company now."

Adam's eyes flared. "That was not how this was supposed to go down."

"What does that mean?" Raine leaned forward. "Do you know something about your father's death?"

Sommers was more direct. "Did you have something to do with your father's death?"

Raine wasn't sure how Adam would react to the insinuation. He would have expected surprise—real or feigned—denial, anger perhaps. He didn't expect curiosity.

Adam's eyes darted around the room, then returned to Raine. "Anything I tell you is secret, right?"

"Right," Raine confirmed. "Anything you tell me is protected by the attorney-client privilege."

Adam pointed at Sommers. "What about her?"

"She's working for me on this case," Raine explained, "so the privilege extends to her."

Raine was already thinking about where Laura kept the criminal fee agreement, how much of a retainer to charge for a murder case. It would actually be a murder investigation case until and unless Kavendish figured it out and arrested Adam. Adam might have the resources to post the standard million-dollar bail the courts usually imposed on a murder case. But Raine would want to get the fee up front, just in case Adam couldn't make bail.

"Even crimes?" Adam asked.

"Especially crimes," Raine answered. "What do you think happens in the jail all day? Defendants telling their lawyers they did it, and their lawyers trying to get them out of it anyway."

"What about future crimes?" Adam asked. "Like if I tell you I'm going to commit a crime, can you tell the police so they'll stop me?"

"Are you planning on committing a crime in the future?" Raine felt compelled to ask.

"Just answer my question, please," Adam replied.

"Well, it depends," Raine started in typically lawyer-like fashion. "The rule says if a client is going to do something that is reasonably certain to result in death or serious bodily injury, then I'm required to disclose it to try to save that person. If it's any other crime, or if it's going to substantially impact somebody's financial standing, then it's discretionary. I don't have to disclose it, but if I do, it's not a violation of the ethics rules."

Adam put a hand to his lips and nodded. Then he just sat there in thought.

Eventually, Sommers cleared her throat and looked at Raine.

"So," Raine prompted, "did you have something to do with your father's death?"

Adam's head popped up again. "What? Oh, no, of course not."

"Of course not?" Raine asked. "After all that?"

Adam shrugged. "Of course not. So, anyway, Mark owns the company now?"

Raine looked to Sommers, and they exchanged puzzled glances. Raine wasn't convinced, but he didn't think he would get anything further out of Adam just then. He elected to go ahead and answer his client's question.

"Well, not quite now," Raine said. "In four days."

"Four days?" Adam and Sommers asked in unison.

"Well, to be perfectly accurate," Raine checked the clock, "it will be your brother's company in one hundred and two hours, give or take a few minutes, depending on when the medical examiner set the time of death."

Sommers cocked her head at him. "What the hell are you talking about?"

Adam pointed at Sommers again. "Yeah. What she said."

Raine suddenly remembered not everyone was a lawyer who was required to take a property law class in law school. "It's called the Survival Rule. If the grantor leaves a bequest to a beneficiary, the bequest doesn't vest until one hundred and twenty hours after the death of the grantor, so if the beneficiary dies within one hundred twenty hours of the grantor, then he is deemed to have predeceased the grantor, and the bequest is void."

Sommers and Adam both blinked at him.

"What?" Sommers asked.

Raine took a deep breath. A big part of his job was explaining complicated legal concepts to laypeople. But property law, and especially estate law, did not lend itself to easy explanation. He was just glad he didn't have to try to explain the Rule Against Perpetuities to them.

"Okay, let me try to say it a different way," Raine offered. "Imagine a situation where an entire family dies all at once in a plane crash. Every one of them has a will, and every one of them leaves their estate to someone else who may or may not also be on the plane. It would be impossible to know who died first, right? It could be a matter of seconds between the deaths, with no real way to figure it out. And if you can't figure out who died in what order, how could you possibly figure out which property passed to who in what order? So to avoid that problem, the law created the Survival Rule. The time amount might vary a little state to state, but basically what the Survival Rule says is that you have to outlive by one hundred and twenty hours the person who died and left you something in their will. If you die within that one-hundred-and-twenty-hour period, then the law declares that you didn't really survive the person who died first after all, not enough anyway, and the will is interpreted as if you died before the person who died first."

"That's ridiculous," Sommers declared. "No wonder everyone hates lawyers."

Raine shrugged. "It probably doesn't need to be a hundred and twenty hours. That's five full days. But I think it serves a purpose if you have someone die and, say, one of their kids dies the next day. It just gives certainty and avoids unnecessary litigation."

"Don't you make money from unnecessary litigation?" Sommers challenged.

Raine just smiled at her. He turned to Adam. "So what that means in this case," he explained, "is that in four days and five hours or so, Mark will have outlived your father sufficiently to inherit the entire company. Then he can do anything he wants with it, and leave it to whomever he wants."

"As long as they outlive him by five days," Adam said.

Raine pointed a finger at him. "Now you're getting it." Then, "So, if you still want to gain control of the company, we can't sue your dad anymore. But we can maybe sue your brother."

Sommers frowned at him.

"I mean, if there's a legal basis," Raine added. "He's probably too young for us to claim he's going senile too."

Adam didn't answer. He picked up his mug and took a long, thoughtful drink. Then he set the mug down again and stood up. "Thank you, Mr. Raine. You've been very helpful. Let me know if there's anything I need to do to settle your account."

"So you won't be challenging your brother's control of the company?" Raine asked as he too stood up. He was hoping to have more hours to bill in a fight against the next challenger to Adam's control of the company, even if he wasn't sure what the basis for that fight would be.

"Hm?" Adam was deep in thought. "Oh, um, I haven't decided exactly what to do about that." He looked at the clock on the wall. "But you said I have a hundred and two hours to decide, is that right?"

"Give or take," Raine qualified.

"Then maybe I'll talk with you after that. Or maybe I won't need to." Adam turned and offered another nod to Sommers. "Ms. Sommers. Mr. Raine. I'll see myself out."

He did so, and Raine rejoined Sommers at the table.

"That Survival Rule is a weird rule," Sommers observed. "I bet it causes more problems than it solves."

Raine considered the Harper family and could only agree.

# 12

Three days later, give or take, Raine and Sawyer met at Delmonico's to either complete their first date, redo it, or have their second date. Raine wasn't sure.

"Does it matter?" Sawyer asked as she opened the door to the restaurant for him.

"Probably not," Raine answered. "I vote we call this our second date."

"Why is that?" Sawyer asked. She had dressed far more femininely for this date. A little black dress and kitten heels, pearls hanging from her wrists and earlobes. Raine found it confusing, but he liked the confusion.

"It means our relationship is progressing," Raine explained.

Sawyer smiled at him, but didn't answer. Instead she turned to the hostess. "Good evening. Table for two, under the name 'Mount'."

Raine had called to ask her on the date. She had already made the dinner reservations.

Their table was in a back corner, dimly lit with candles, a bottle of champagne waiting in a bucket of ice.

"Nice touch." Raine admired the champagne.

"We're not getting drunk at a speakeasy first," Sawyer explained, "so I thought we should make alternative arrangements."

"Always thinking of contingencies." Raine pulled her chair out for her. "The sign of a good lawyer."

"Nah, I just want to drink," Sawyer admitted as she sat down.

She smelled amazing. Not floral or fruity like perfume. Just clean and fresh. Raine felt very fortunate to be right there, right then.

The champagne was good, the food was better, and the conversation was the best. Light, easy, fast, funny. Raine hadn't felt that comfortable with a woman in a very long time. Well before the divorce, he realized. He felt like he could breathe again, and he hadn't even known he wasn't.

The plates were cleared, the bill was paid, and they made their way to the exit. A light rain had started, but it wasn't worth doing anything about. Not by Seattle standards anyway.

"So what now?" Sawyer asked when they stepped outside.

The evening was still relatively young. Raine knew how he wanted the evening to end, but he supposed they should do something else first.

Before he could suggest anything, Sawyer answered her own question. "My apartment is about five blocks away. Let's just go straight there. Right?"

Raine smiled. "Right."

Unlike Bill Harper, when Mark Harper fell to his death

from the scaffolding of the unfinished condo tower across the street from Delmonico's, he screamed the entire way down. But he made approximately the same noise when he struck the ground.

Sawyer looked at Raine. Raine was staring across the street at the construction site.

"Was that what I think it was?" she asked.

Raine nodded.

"Should we jump the fence again?"

Raine shook his head.

Sawyer took a moment. "Do you know who it was?"

Raine nodded. "I wish I didn't."

Sawyer paced in a tight circle, like a tiger in a cage. She obviously wanted to do something, but there wasn't anything to do. And the mood was definitely ruined. Finally she stopped and shoved her fists on her hips. "Our dates suck."

———

RAINE NEEDED confirmation that the second victim was indeed Mark Harper. That meant waiting around for the cops. Sawyer was not interested in anything to do with police officers. They parted company with a vague agreement to try again soon.

"Third time's the charm," one of them had offered weakly, although Raine already couldn't remember if he or Sawyer had said it.

The flame wasn't quite out, but the window was open, and the candle was flickering. So he did what he always did when a relationship started to feel unsecure. He retreated into his work. Natalie had finally had enough of it. Maybe it was better, Raine told himself, if Sawyer never had to reach that point. It wasn't like she would have any shortage of suitors. Maybe he wasn't as ready for a new relationship as he'd thought. Maybe—

"Mr. Raine?" It was Detective Kavendish again, mercifully interrupting Raine's runaway thoughts. "I'm starting to think you might be a suspect after all. How is it you came to be at the scene of this death as well?"

Raine gestured across the street. "Delmonico's. Ms. Mount and I tried to recreate our first date."

Kavendish looked up at Harper Tower, then down at the ground where they both knew someone had fallen to their death. Again. "You might have recreated it a little too well."

"Was it Mark Harper?" Raine just went ahead and asked. He didn't have it in him to play dumb and try to extract information from Kavendish without the detective realizing what Raine was doing. That was an art, and art took effort. Raine wanted to go home.

Kavendish frowned at Raine. His expression betrayed his thoughts, at least to an experienced lawyer whose practice included criminal defense. Facts from an investigation were confidential from the public. But it wasn't unheard of for a detective to tell a suspect select information during an interrogation in order to convince the suspect that the police already had all the evidence they needed to prove he was guilty. Disclosure of investigatory information was discretionary in the detective. They both knew that. They also both knew the answer to Raine's question.

Kavendish nodded. "How did you know that?"

"The Survival Rule," Raine answered.

Kavendish frowned again. A cop wouldn't know a legal principle from wills and estates. "Like, survival of the fittest?"

Raine shook his head. "Survival of the most informed."

## 13

R aine and Kavendish had both said too much. Raine terminated the conversation; Kavendish let him. Sawyer was long gone, so Raine went home and tried to get some sleep before he ambushed Adam Harper outside the secure building that housed his top-floor condominium. Raine knew he couldn't get inside without a pass card. But he could wait on the bench outside the front door. Well, after the man who'd slept on it all night gathered up his things and moved down the street to wherever his next shelter would be. Raine regarded the bench for several seconds, then decided to stand after all.

Twenty-three minutes later, Adam bounded out of the lobby, looking far happier than a man whose father and brother had just died less than a hundred and twenty hours apart should have looked.

"Adam," Raine called out. It wasn't a shout, but there was force to his voice.

Adam turned around. When he saw Raine, his expression morphed from curiosity to disappointment. "What are you doing here? Is there some other stupid rule that will keep me from inheriting my family business?"

"If I say yes," Raine responded, "is someone else going to die?"

Adam crossed his arms. "What are you talking about?" It was busy on the sidewalk. Adam wasn't the only one on his way to start his day, and the homeless man who had scurried away upon Raine's arrival wasn't the only member of the city's homeless population retreating to less patrolled areas after spreading out to useable sleeping places during the night. It was like a changing of the guard, the good people of the world taking over from the less fortunate. Except the particular person Raine had come to see didn't seem like such a good person after all.

"Can we go somewhere more private?" Raine asked. "I have some questions about your brother's death."

Adam frowned. "You know about that already? Of course you do. You probably predicted it."

"I didn't," Raine assured him. "I didn't think you would actually do anything like that."

Adam raised his chin and looked down his nose at Raine. "Like what?" he demanded.

Raine looked around again at the rapidly increasing number of people on the street around them. "We should go someplace private. Anything you say to me is confidential under the attorney-client privilege, but the privilege is waived if you talk where third parties can hear you."

"Attorney-client privilege?" Adam shook his head. "I don't think I need a lawyer anymore. What was that word you used the other day? Oh, yeah. 'Moot'. Whatever you were doing for me, it's moot now. The company is mine now. Well, it will be at seven tonight, one hundred twenty hours after Dad died. The thing I hired you to do, it happened without you. So thanks for nothing."

"I'm the one who told you about the Survival Rule," Raine reminded him. "But seriously, let's move this inside to somewhere where we can close the door. It doesn't take a rocket scientist to put two and two together. You may not need me to take your dad's company away from him, but don't be surprised if you need me when the cops come to take your freedom away from you."

"The cops?" Adam was incredulous. "You think I committed murder, but you still want to be my lawyer. No wonder everyone hates lawyers."

"Not everyone hates lawyers." Raine felt the need to defend his profession.

"Everyone except other lawyers," Adam suggested. "Look, if you think I did it, why would I tell you? You'll just go tell the cops."

Raine shook his head. "No, like I told you before, everything we talk about is protected. Defendants need to be able to tell their lawyers the truth without fear that what they say will get out somehow. Attorneys are ethically obligated not to tell anyone anything about anything discussed with a client."

"Unless it's on a busy sidewalk." Adam seemed to finally understand.

"Exactly." Raine pointed an approving finger at him.

Adam pointed back. "I don't care if anyone hears what I'm about to say. I didn't kill my father, and I didn't kill my brother. But I will take the company from them. And I don't need your help to do that anymore."

Raine sighed. He couldn't force a client to talk to him. He

would just wait until Adam talked to someone he shouldn't. Then he was very likely to need a lawyer again.

"Fine," Raine said. "Just don't talk to the cops."

"Wouldn't that make me look guilty?" Adam questioned.

"Not as guilty as they'll make you look if you do talk to them," Raine warned.

Adam sighed. "Is there anything useful you can actually do for me? If not, then—"

"You'll need to probate the estate," Raine answered. "It's not very interesting, but you will want to make sure everything goes where it's supposed to. You won't be able to exercise control over the company until that's completed. I can guide it through the probate court."

"Will that be faster than if I do it myself?" Adam asked.

"Uh, yes," Raine answered. "This is a substantial estate with a lot of different types of assets. I can make it go as fast as possible."

Adam narrowed his eyes slightly. "Same hourly rate?"

"Same billable hourly rate," Raine confirmed. "It'll be a lot less than the lawsuit you originally filed would have been."

"Fine." Adam waved a hand at him. "Probate the will or whatever. Just get me control of my dad's—I mean, my company as soon as possible."

"Okay," Raine said. "I'll draft up a new fee agreement, and—"

"Ugh!" Adam sighed. "Can you just email it to me or something? I'm a very busy man. Very important now. Have your person send it to my people, and I will sign it when I get the chance."

"And I'll start working on it once you sign it," Raine said, "and refill your retainer account."

## 14

It took Adam over a week to get the signed fee agreement and the money to Raine. The delay might seem to belie Adam's claim that he wanted things done as soon as possible, but Raine knew what Adam meant was that he wanted everyone else to do their tasks as soon as possible. He would join in when he could. After all, he was "very important now".

In the meantime, construction on Harper Tower had ground to a halt. Until the probate was complete, Adam wouldn't have legal control over any of the firm's assets. That meant he couldn't pay the workers or the subcontractors or the banks. All of the things Bill Harper had warned Judge Malloy about. Raine figured those people would be Adam's problem, and the desire not to deal with them might be motivation to start the probate of the estate, but as much as Bill Harper was concerned about his ability to pay his workers, that was how uninterested Adam seemed to be about it.

Raine decided it wasn't really his problem as long as he got paid. The will would be probated in due course, and then Raine could move on to the next client. Unless Kavendish arrested Adam. Raine frowned at the prospect as he walked into his office a few mornings later. He really didn't like criminal defense. Maybe he could refer the case to Sawyer. Which reminded him, he really needed to ask her out on another date. He wasn't exactly sure why he hadn't yet. But then again, she hadn't reached out to him. Which was part of the reason he hadn't reached out to her. Vicious circle.

"Mr. Raine?" A woman in his lobby stood up as he entered the office. Laura had already provided her with an intake sheet and a cup of tea.

"That's me," Raine confirmed. He extended a hand. "And you are?"

"Meredith Wilcox," the woman answered. She was in her early forties, with shoulder-length brown hair, light makeup, and a few straggling gray hairs.

Raine recognized the name, but he couldn't place it. His face must have communicated his uncertainty.

"I'm a friend of Rebecca Sommers's," Wilcox explained. "She said I could talk to you about the Harper Tower project."

Raine remembered. "You own an HVAC business, right?"

Wilcox smiled. "Right. Rebecca must have told you."

"She also told me that Bill Harper terminated your contract without cause," Raine said, "but if you want to sue him, you're too late. He's dead."

"I know," Wilcox said. "Everyone knows that. No, I came to you because you're Adam's lawyer. I'm hoping you might convince him to pay me for the work I did before the project goes bankrupt."

"Bankrupt?" Raine was surprised by that suggestion.

"Well, maybe not formal bankruptcy," Wilcox qualified, "but no one expects Adam to complete the project."

"He can't just leave a half-complete skyscraper in the middle of downtown Seattle," Raine said.

"Actually, he can," Wilcox returned. "He has to finish the outside so it's not an eyesore, but he doesn't have to finish the interior if the project collapses. Half the office space in Seattle is empty right now, but you wouldn't know it looking at the completed exteriors of all the new buildings."

Raine shook his head. "Why would he fight so hard to get control of the company if the first thing he does is shut down their latest and greatest project?"

"That's the sixty-five-million-dollar question," Wilcox said. "Well, not that much, actually. But I would like to get paid. Do you think you can help me with that?"

"I can't sue Adam for you," Raine answered. "I can't sue my own client. That's a pretty clear conflict of interest."

"I suppose it would be," Wilcox agreed.

Wilcox thanked Raine for his time, shook his hand, and set the intake form down on her seat. She wasn't going to be a new client. Adam had tied him up for any case related to Harper Development and Harper Tower. Which reminded Raine of what Sommers had said about her friend Meredith Wilcox.

"Before you leave, Ms. Wilcox," Raine said, "could I ask you one question?"

"Of course." Wilcox stopped just next to the door.

"When Bill Harper came to your office and terminated your contract," Raine said, "did you notice anything about him that might suggest some sort of mental infirmity?"

"You mean did he seem senile like Adam hired you to

say?" Wilcox knew the real question. "Rebecca told me what the lawsuit was."

"Ah." Raine nodded. "Well, yes. Did you see anything like that?"

"You know," Wilcox took a deep breath before answering, "I dealt with Bill Harper a lot over the last ten years or so. He was rude, cheap, ruthless, borderline dishonest, and quick to anger. But he was not senile. When Rebecca told me what Adam was claiming, I couldn't believe it. You never would have won that case. Adam got lucky when his dad fell off that building."

*And then his brother*, Raine thought, but decided not to voice it. He didn't want to explain the Survival Rule again.

"He must have been desperate about something," Wilcox remarked.

"Why desperate?" Raine asked.

"Well, claiming something he knew wasn't true was almost certain to fail," Wilcox explained, "but he did it anyway. As hopeless as that course of action was, there must have been something he feared more if he didn't do it."

Raine thought that was a very astute observation. "Thank you, Ms. Wilcox. I hope I can convince Adam to pay you for your services rendered."

"I hope so too," Wilcox replied. "Rebecca said you're a really good attorney. I have faith in you."

Wilcox exited the office, and Raine was left with the mystery of what Adam Harper feared more than filing a guaranteed loser of a lawsuit against his own father. And the fact that Sommers thought he was a really good attorney. That was nice to know.

## 15

"**I** swear, Dan," Sommers told him a few days later, "you are the worst attorney ever sometimes."

So much for Sommers's alleged adulation of him.

"Well, not the worst," she corrected. "Least fun."

"Least fun attorney?" Raine said. "I think there a lot of lawyers in the running for that."

"Least... adventurous," Sommers tried again.

Raine crossed his arms and stared at his sometimes partner. "What do you want to do?"

It all made sense then. Sommers had shown up unannounced at exactly 4:40. Twenty minutes was the perfect amount of time to engage in small talk until 5:00 arrived and the real reason for the visit could be revealed. Raine had to admire Sommers's people-management skills, even when she used them on him.

"It's not what I want to do," Sommers answered. "It's what you need to do."

"Don't throw a sales pitch at me, Rebecca," Raine said. "You're not selling a condo to me."

"I'm not selling a condo to anyone," Sommers sneered. "I do commercial real estate. But you make an important point. No one is selling condos to you or anyone else, not from the Harper Tower, anyway."

"Yeah, I'm hearing it might shut down without getting completed," Raine said. "Bill was a jackass, but Adam just doesn't seem to care."

"Doesn't that seem weird," Sommers asked, "given all the things he did to get the company?"

"Like the lawsuit?" Raine asked.

"That, of course," Sommers confirmed. "But what about his dad and brother? Two accidents, back-to-back like that."

"And after I told him he would inherit everything," Raine added, "if his brother died in the next four days. I feel kind of guilty about that."

"You should," Sommers teased. "But you should also do something about it."

"What?"

Sommers placed a hand on her chin. "I'm not entirely sure."

Raine knew that was a lie. "Is it going to involve committing any crimes?"

"It's not a crime if they don't catch you," Sommers answered. "Didn't you learn that when you were a kid?"

Raine thought for a moment. "No, I never learned that."

Sommers offered a tight grin. "I guess you and I had very different childhoods."

Raine suddenly realized he didn't know nearly as much about Sommers as he probably should. Especially given what she was proposing. Still, he trusted her.

"Fine," he said. "But let's wait until after dark. I don't

want to get caught trespassing inside that construction site again."

"I just told you, Dan," Sommers chided, "it's not trespassing if you don't get caught."

---

DARK CAME WITH WET. There was a steady rain by the time Raine and Sommers reached the Harper Tower construction site. It also wasn't an even distribution of dark and wet. It was definitely wet, but the streetlights all over downtown made the area considerably less dark than Raine would have preferred. Sommers seemed indifferent.

"What are we looking for, again?" Raine asked as they reached the locked gate. They had added barbed wire to the top of it since he and Sawyer had traversed it. They would need a different way inside.

"Clues," Sommers answered.

Raine waited for more, but there was none. "Clues?" he repeated incredulously. "Like we're a group of teenage mystery solvers?"

"It's been a long time since I was a teenager," Sommers said. "Even longer for you."

Raine frowned, but she wasn't wrong.

"Okay, a pair of middle-aged mystery solvers," Raine amended. "Can you be more specific?"

"Yes, I want to know whether there was anyone else here the nights Bill Harper and Mark Harper died," Sommers answered.

"You think Adam was here?"

"I think it's possible someone was here," Sommers

answered carefully. "And if there was someone here, I think it's possible it was Adam."

"How concrete," Raine scoffed. "Speaking of concrete, I wonder if they've replaced the pavement yet. It's definitely going to be stained by those bodies."

"Gross." Sommers stuck out her tongue.

Raine shrugged. "At least you didn't see Old Man Harper immediately after he hit that pavement. Now, that was gross."

Sommers grimaced. Raine felt some small satisfaction from that.

"So how do we get inside?" Raine brought himself back to the task at hand. "We're not getting over that barbed wire."

Sommers's expression brightened again. She grinned and beckoned him with a finger. "Follow me."

Sommers began to walk quickly around the perimeter of the construction site, which was an entire city block. The fingers of her inside hand skimmed across the wire fencing, occasionally grabbing a portion of the fence only to let go again almost immediately. Raine wondered what she was doing, but she was going so fast, he didn't have a chance to ask her. Finally, on the opposite side of the site from the barbed-wired gate, Sommers found their way in. She pulled at the fence, and a section separated from the one next to it more than large enough to slip through.

"I sell a lot of commercial property before it's even finished," Sommers explained. "Clients want to see the construction site at least before they commit. Residential agents go into empty homes uninvited. I go into empty commercial buildings the same way."

"Those homes usually have a key box at the front door,"

Raine pointed out. "This place has an eight-foot-tall perimeter fence and a hundred 'No Trespassing' signs."

"Details." Sommers waved a dismissive hand at Raine. "There's a reason one section of the fence can be pulled apart."

"You think that's for you?" Raine asked. "Not just that the fence person that day forgot to connect them fully?"

"It's for me now, Dan," Sommers answered. "Just like it was for me all the other times I needed to get a peek at the retail shop spaces on the first floor so I could close a deal and continue to be Seattle's Number One Commercial Real Estate Agent."

"Downtown core and First Hill," Raine added. "So, is that our cover story if we get caught?"

"What? No!" Sommers scoffed. "Confessing to trespassing is not a cover story. Our cover story is that you're the lawyer to the new company president and needed to check out something at the site."

"Check out what?" Raine asked.

"It doesn't matter," Sommers said.

"I don't want to be making something up when the cops nab us," he complained.

"Then don't get nabbed," Sommers suggested before slipping between the fence sections and disappearing inside.

Raine sighed, then followed her into the worksite. "Tax records or something," he told himself on the way. "Something boring so the cops won't even want to hear about them, let alone see any proof. Maybe permits. Construction people are always talking about pulling permits."

Sommers was standing on the other side of the fence. It was considerably darker inside the construction site, that eight-foot-fence blocking a lot of the ambient light from the street. The good news was that they were inside. The bad news was that the impact site of Bill Harper, and maybe Mark Harper, was on the opposite side of the worksite.

"Watch out for nails," Sommers warned, pointing at the ground.

Raine had changed out of his suit, but he didn't own a pair of steel-toed work boots. Any stray nails would be more than able to pierce the sole of his sneakers. He appreciated the warning from Sommers. Maybe she had done this before. He had assumed she was exaggerating to get him to go along with the plan.

About halfway to their destination, Raine saw something that caught his eye. He reached out and tapped Sommers on the shoulder. Then pointed at the elevator affixed to the side of the building. "I bet that's how they got up to the nineteenth floor. Let's check it out."

"The nineteenth floor?" Sommers croaked. "The unfinished floor from which two experienced construction magnates fell to their deaths? That doesn't seem like a great idea."

"I bet that's where the best clues are," Raine countered. "If we're doing this, let's do it right."

They were definitely doing it, so Sommers agreed, and they made their way to the elevator.

When they got there, Raine frowned. "You need a pass card," he observed.

"That's too bad," Sommers replied.

"But there's a bright side," Raine added.

"What's that?" Sommers asked.

Raine nodded at the pad where the elevator riders would flash their badges. "I bet the elevator keeps track of everyone who flashed their badge. There are probably records of who went up to the nineteenth floor on the dates of the murder."

"Can we get those?" Sommers asked.

Raine frowned. "We could ask, but that would tip off anyone who might have been involved."

"Adam," Sommers said, "Adam is the one who might have been involved."

Raine nodded. "Agreed. So, as the president of the company, he would definitely be in a position to know if I subpoenaed the records."

"Subpoena?" Sommers laughed. "Why would you use a subpoena?"

"Well, it's a private business, not a government agency," Raine tried to explain, "so I can't do a public records request."

The elevator turned out to be more of a dead end than a clue, but it was something they could return to if they got desperate enough. They returned to their circumnavigation of the construction site and after a few moments and absolutely no nails through either of their shoes, they arrived at the cement plaza in front of the main entrance. It was definitely stained.

And there were definitely two stains. One on top of the other.

"Did they hit the same spot?" Sommers observed.

"They did," Raine agreed.

"That's a clue," Sommers declared.

Raine rubbed his chin. "I wonder why Mark jumped from the exact same spot as his father."

"You think it was a suicide?" Sommers asked. "Not an accident?"

Raine nodded at the overlapping stains. "The first one

could have been anything. Accident, suicide, homicide. But the location of the second stain, it shows Mark's death was intentional."

"Suicide?" Sommers suggested.

"Or homicide," Raine considered. He frowned. "Probably homicide."

"Probably your client," Sommers added.

"Probably," Raine agreed. "That's awkward."

"Hello?" a deep, raspy voice called out from the dark. "Is there someone here?"

"Oh shit!" Sommers whispered, dropping into a crouch.

Raine followed suit, and he began scanning for exits. The way they entered was too far away. And in case he wasn't entirely sure, the next sound they heard was that of a dog barking.

"They have a guard dog now?" Raine shook his head at the development.

"I guess a couple of deaths at your construction site would justify that," Sommers suggested. She gestured to the locked and barbed-wired gate that Raine and Sawyer had jumped back when it was only a locked gate. "There's our way out."

"Barbed wire," Raine pointed out.

"It's tipped toward the street," Sommers explained. "You can climb over it from this side."

Raine frowned at her. "Is that true?"

"We really did have different childhoods." Sommers grinned at him. "On three."

"You go first," Raine said. "We can't both go over at the same time."

"It's going to be loud when I hit it," Sommers argued. "You need to be right behind me."

Raine nodded.

"If there's someone here, come out and show yourself," the security guard called out. "Don't make me sic the dog on you."

"Ready?" Sommers asked, already leaning into her imminent sprint to the gate.

"Hold on." Raine scanned the ground and found a small hunk of concrete, about the size of a softball. He stood, nodded to Sommers, then threw it as far from their position as he could.

A few seconds later it landed with an underwhelming thud, but it was enough to draw attention away from them. The dog started barking like crazy, and the human yelled out another warning, his voice trailing toward where the chunk had landed.

"Go!" Raine whisper-yelled, and the two of them sprinted toward the gate.

Sommers was surprisingly fast and leaped onto the chain-link gate from several feet away, sending it shaking with a cacophony of aluminum and steel rattling against each other.

"Stop!" the security guard called out. He wasn't far enough away. The dog's barking grew frenzied, and Raine heard the man command, "Sic 'em!"

He scrambled up the fence even as the dog closed the distance between his handler and the trespassers in less time than it took Raine to reach the barbed wire. He definitely could navigate up and over it more easily than if it had been tipped back toward him, but it was still covered in sharp metal barbs. The dog leaped onto the gate in a fashion remarkably similar to Sommers. Raine pulled his feet up instinctively, causing him to lose his balance and reach out for the nearest thing: the barbed wire. One barb sliced open the side of his left index finger. Another barb punctured the palm of his right hand.

"Ow! Fuck!" he couldn't help but yell, but it wasn't like he was giving away their position.

"Stop! Stop!" The security guard was almost to the gate as well, where his dog was jumping repeatedly at Raine, who had hesitated after injuring his hands.

Raine scrambled over the rest of the barbed wire, shredding a pant leg and the shin underneath. He jumped to the sidewalk, sending shock waves through his knees, which were very definitely too old for this; then he pulled himself to his feet and bolted toward the waterfront. If there was anywhere a soaking wet, bleeding, limping man could blend in, it would be with the transients who had taken over most of Third Avenue. He doubted the dog or his handler would pursue them outside the worksite, but he wasn't certain either.

Sommers was nowhere to be seen. She had run off in some unknown direction, again faster than Raine would have guessed, and certainly faster than he could match given his injuries.

Did she really escape unscathed? he wondered.

Then, as his right hand began throbbing, he wondered where the nearest urgent care clinic was. And when his last tetanus shot was.

## 16

"What happened to your hand?" Natalie asked when she opened her front door and saw the bandage on Raine's hand.

"Punctured it climbing over a barbed-wire fence," he told her.

Her mouth twisted into a crooked frown, and she shook her head. "If you don't want to tell me, just say so. Don't lie to me."

"If I was going to lie," Raine responded, "I would have said I was fighting off a werewolf. That's way cooler than barbed wire."

"What's cooler than barbed wire?" Jordan asked, joining the conversation late as he slipped past his mom to head to Raine's car.

Raine held his bandaged hand aloft. "I fought off a werewolf."

Jason just rolled his eyes at his father as he exited the house, backpack over one shoulder and earbuds in his ears but apparently at a low enough volume to allow him to hear and react to the mortifying things his father said.

"Oh, I thought it was something real," Jordan said in reply to Raine's werewolf claim. Then he joined his brother in the car.

"They used to like me," Raine insisted to his ex-wife.

"There's a lot of that going around," she replied.

Raine's expression dropped.

Natalie reached out for him. "Oh, I'm sorry, Dan. I didn't mean it like that. It was just a joke. It sounded a lot worse than I meant."

The stab to the heart Raine felt at Natalie's joke was momentary. He couldn't help but feel it, but he could choose not to linger in it. "No worries, Nat. It was funny. I'll drop them off Friday night."

"Okay, thanks," Natalie replied. Her frown had untwisted from disapproval with Raine to disapproval with herself. "Um, how's work going?"

Raine, who had already started to turn toward his car, froze in mid-step. She never asked about his work. Even when they were married. Work was for work. When he got home, it was time to take care of the kids.

"Uhh..." he stammered. "Fine. It's good. Yeah, good. Just more lawyer stuff, you know. Suing people and releasing criminals to keep the lights on."

Natalie nodded along, waited a beat, then asked, "Did you run into Zac Chapman again?"

That stab to the heart was more than just momentary. "No," he lied. "I just saw him that one time."

If she knew he was lying, it was because she had already reached out to Chapman. But she'd have to admit that in order to call him out on his lie.

"Oh," was all she said. "Well, okay then. Have fun with the boys this week."

"I will," Raine answered. He tried to look into Natalie's eyes, but she avoided eye contact. So he turned again and walked to his car, wishing several things. He wished he didn't care if Natalie was seeing other men. He wished he didn't care that one of those men might be Zac Chapman. And he wished he still had a case against Chapman so he could kick his ass up and down the courtroom.

## 17

Once his blood cooled, Raine realized he also wished he had called Sawyer sooner about trying a third time to have a first date. By the time he got around to it, he got voicemail. When he texted her, he was left on "read". He'd missed his shot. It made him dislike Adam Harper even more than he already did. If it hadn't been for the raining of dead Harpers, Raine was certain he and Sawyer would be officially dating. If that was what people called it anymore.

Raine was going to be glad to get the probate finished. It wasn't sexy work. It wasn't even interesting. No juries, no opening statements, no closing arguments. It was just Raine presenting orders to a judge to sign in order to effectuate what Old Man Harper had written in his very last will and testament.

At least Raine was able to bill some hours, and Adam had filled his retainer account before all but disappearing, so Raine could get paid, unlike Meredith Wilcox and untold numbers of workers and contractors who got stiffed when construction on the Harper Tower ground to a halt upon the death of the two Harpers who actually wanted to complete the construction, apparently. Raine would be glad to be done with this last aspect of his representation of Adam Harper. It had been financially favorable, but after everything that had happened, there was nothing that could make him glad he had trudged up to the King County Courthouse again.

Almost nothing.

"Dan?"

Raine recognized the voice behind him in the hallway outside the clerk's office. He spun around more eagerly than he wished he had, to see Sawyer Mount radiating sunlight in the otherwise dank corridor. Her blonde hair was slicked back from her face; she was wearing a men's suit jacket and a pleated A-line skirt, with several strands of pearls around her neck, and dark wine-colored lipstick.

"Sawyer," he replied as evenly as he could muster. He was experiencing a lot of conflicting emotions. Joy at seeing her, anger that she had ghosted him, embarrassment, shame, and something else he couldn't quite identify but he was pretty sure he hadn't felt since high school. He didn't like it, and he determined to act like a man of his age, not a teenager seeing his crush on the way to gym class.

"I was hoping I would run into you here," she said.

Raine added confusion to the mix of emotions. And, despite himself, hope. "You were?"

"Of course!" She extracted a phone from her jacket. "I lost my phone. I didn't have your contact info saved anywhere. I'm still hoping we can make that third time a charm, if you know what I mean."

He definitely did know what she meant. And all of those emotions melted into a single, calm, more than manageable sensation of happiness. He jabbed a thumb toward the café. "Can I buy you a cup of coffee, Ms. Mount?"

"I would like that very much, Mr. Raine," she replied with the brightest smile Raine could ever remember seeing. At least since the last time he'd seen her smile.

"How did you lose your phone?" Raine asked when they reached the café.

"You're not going to believe this." Sawyer shook her head solemnly. "I lost it fighting off a brood of vampires."

Raine stared at her for several long moments. Then, just as it was getting too weird, he raised his still-bandaged hand. "Werewolves."

Sawyer nodded approvingly. "Nice. I'm glad we're on the same page with this sort of thing."

"Of course," Raine replied. "People like us, we have to stick together."

Sawyer smiled again. "I like the sound of that."

They ordered their drinks and sat at the only available table, a small wobbly one that was a little close to the main hallway, so that people were constantly walking right next to them. Raine couldn't have cared less. Sawyer didn't mind either.

"As long as we don't have dead bodies literally falling around us, I'm good," she assured him. "Speaking of which, I vote that we go somewhere other than Delmonico's for our third first date. In fact, let's avoid any restaurants within three blocks of that construction site."

"Three blocks?" Raine questioned.

"Better safe than sorry," Sawyer offered.

Raine had no argument with the three-block suggestion, but before he could confirm as much, Zac Chapman walked by their table, practically brushing against Sawyer. He didn't seem to notice Raine, but Raine couldn't help but notice him, despite himself. He watched after him for a moment too long.

"Who's that?" Sawyer asked. "A friend of yours?"

"More like the opposite of that," Raine said as he pulled his gaze back to his companion.

"Ooh, spill." Sawyer leaned forward. "I think it's important to have a nemesis. I make a point of having at least one person I hate at any given time."

"Wow," was all Raine could think to say.

"So why do you hate that guy?"

Raine wasn't about to talk to Sawyer about his ex-wife and a past and renewed rival for her affections. "First, I don't hate him."

"You're lying," Sawyer interjected. "I mean, I understand why you think you're supposed to say that, but I really would prefer it if you didn't lie to me."

Raine considered that for a moment. "Okay. Well, among other things, he was opposing counsel on the case against Bill Harper."

"The dead guy!" Sawyer remembered the name. "Well, the first dead guy."

"Yeah, that case," Raine confirmed.

"Dude lost a case because his client fell out of a building?" Sawyer laughed. "That's rough."

"Well, technically, the case became moot at that point," Raine clarified. "I didn't win because there wasn't anyone to beat anymore."

Sawyer nodded toward where Chapman had walked to. "Beat that guy."

"I'd like to, but the case is over." Raine shrugged. "I'm just doing some cleanup, walking it through probate."

"That sounds oppressively dull," Sawyer commented.

"It is," Raine agreed, "but it's paying the bills right now."

Before they could talk further about the case, Chapman suddenly appeared again next to their table. "Raine," he said in greeting.

"Chapman." Raine returned the greeting.

"Nemesis," Sawyer added.

That confused Chapman, especially when Raine laughed. A moment later he regained himself and shoved a raft of papers at Raine. "You are served."

Raine took the papers and read the caption aloud. "Sarah Harper, Petitioner, versus Adam Harper, Respondent. Motion to Contest Last Will and Testament of William Harper."

"See you in court, Raine," Chapman growled.

"Woohoo!" Sawyer threw her hands up. "Fight! Fight! Fight!"

## 18

"I don't understand." Adam stared at the copy of the will challenge Raine had handed him. "You said Mark had to outlive Dad by five days. He didn't. I get everything. Did you lie to me?"

It was another impromptu client meeting, after another unexpected event. At least no one died this time. This one was taking place in Adam's condominium. He wasn't answering his phone anymore, and he had stopped going to the construction site. Everyone had stopped going there. It was a ghost town. With at least two ghosts.

So Raine had staked out Adam's residence again, knowing he was likely to step out at some point to get dinner. The only risk was if he ordered delivery or cooked at home. He didn't seem like the kind of person who cooked for himself. And Raine was prepared to sneak in behind the delivery guy, if it came to that. Fortunately, Adam stepped outside a little after 6:00, and Raine started the conversation by shoving Chapman's motion in his face and declaring, "You're about to lose everything!" Five minutes later they were upstairs in Adam's penthouse. Adam poured himself a drink in lieu of dinner. He didn't offer one to Raine.

Raine rubbed the back of his neck. "I didn't lie to you," he insisted.

That was the problem with being a lawyer. People hired you to tell them what the law was. But they also hired you to get a specific result, whether the law supported it or not.

"Sarah is asking the court to ignore the law," he explained. "She has the right to contest the will, but that doesn't mean she'll win."

"Isn't this a frivolous lawsuit?" Adam demanded. "Can she get charged with a crime for filing this? False reporting or something?"

Raine really wished he had that drink Adam didn't offer him.

"It's not a crime to file a frivolous lawsuit," Raine answered. "False reporting is calling 911 and reporting a fire that hasn't happened or a crime that never took place. The most you can get for filing a frivolous lawsuit is being forced to pay the other side's legal fees for wasting their time."

"Let's do that!" Adam pointed at him.

"We can definitely ask," Raine allowed. "I don't really care how I'm paid, although I'm sure you do."

"I'd love to make Sarah pay your bill." Adam laughed. "How dare she challenge me? I earned this, fair and square."

Raine wondered about the word "earned". He decided not to ask. Not right then, anyway. But he suspected Adam's role, if any, would be a central issue in Sarah's lawsuit.

"Why don't we avoid the word 'earned'?" Raine suggested. "We'll do better to play the role of fortunate bene-ficiary, inheriting by happenstance, but determined to make the most of this opportunity for the future of the family business and the lasting legacy of your father."

Adam blinked at Raine. "That's good. That's really good."

Raine allowed a small smile. "Thank you."

"Yeah, keep talking like that," Adam encouraged with a roll of his hand. "How can we lose?"

Raine could think of several ways. That was also what lawyers got hired for—anticipating the other side's moves. He stood up and crossed the room to the picture window, looking out at Elliott Bay. He clasped his hands behind his back and took in the panoramic view of the city from the lofty heights above the crime and poverty tucked into the alleys below.

"I'm going to need one of those drinks you poured for yourself," he said without turning around.

"I'm sorry?" Adam stammered.

"Please pour me a drink, Adam," Raine repeated, finally turning back to his client. "What you're having is fine."

Adam looked at his glass. "This is top-shelf stuff," he protested.

"And I'm a top-shelf attorney," Raine replied. "That's why you sought me out."

"I sought you out because every other lawyer in town had a conflict of interest," Adam said. "If you were that top-shelf, we would have already used you somewhere along the way."

Raine frowned slightly. "I've done well for you so far. You're this close to getting control of your father's company."

"Only because every time it looked like we were going to lose," Adam protested, "a gift fell into your lap."

Raine's frown deepened. He couldn't ignore Adam's

choice of words anymore. But that drink would help the conversation he was about to start.

"Let's talk about that," Raine agreed. "But let's do it like gentlemen. Over fine whiskey, with nothing held back."

Adam took a moment, then shook his head. "Fine. I suppose I can spare an ounce. But you should know that one ounce of this costs more than you charge for an entire hour."

Raine didn't doubt it. He also didn't say anything more until he had the ounce in his hand.

"Now," he said, returning to his seat on Adam's couch, "shall we talk about the ways you could lose this case, and the gifts that fell into my lap? They're not unrelated."

Adam narrowed his eyes at his lawyer, then sat down in the chair opposite him, a glass coffee table between them. "What is that supposed to mean?"

Raine picked up the motion to contest the will, which Adam had dropped on the coffee table after little more than a cursory review of the caption. "There are only two ways we lose this case, and Sarah is asserting both of them. The first one is straightforward. She is arguing that the one-hundred-and-twenty-hour rule is unconscionable."

"Unconscionable?" Adam sneered at the word. "What does that mean?"

"It's a lawyer word that judges use when the law is clear but they don't want to enforce it," Raine explained. "Sarah is arguing that applying the rule strictly would result in a miscarriage of justice. Your father left everything to Mark in his will. In Mark's will, he left everything to Sarah. So what should have happened is that everything goes from your dad to her, via Mark. That was your dad's intent and Mark's intent, so applying some arcane rule would frustrate what they wanted. And there's plenty of case law that courts are supposed to try to effectuate the underlying intent of the will."

"My dad would never have intended for the family business to go to someone outside of the family," Adam argued.

Raine tipped his glass of whiskey at Adam. "A very good point, and one we will be sure to make. But there is also evidence that your father would never have intended for the family business to go to you. At least not after you sued him."

"He left me in the will, at least as a backup," Adam pointed out. "He knew it was a possibility."

"And he knew it was a possibility Sarah would get everything eventually," Raine countered. "They didn't have any kids. Mark was likely to leave everything to her in his will."

Adam frowned. "You're sounding very pessimistic right now. Maybe you aren't the right lawyer for this case after all."

"I'm your lawyer, not your cheerleader," Raine told him. "You literally just asked, 'How could we lose?' So I'm telling you. That's the best way to avoid it happening."

Adam pushed himself back in his chair and huffed.

"But that argument isn't our biggest worry," Raine continued. He started to set his drink down, but then couldn't quite let it go. It really was top-shelf. He took another sip, let it linger in his mouth, then swallowed. "It's difficult to prevail on a request to ignore settled law. Unless..."

"Unless what?" Adam stood up, arms crossed, drink still in one hand.

"Unless the other party has unclean hands."

"Unclean hands?" Adam wrinkled his nose at the expression. "What does that mean? And why don't you lawyers just use plain English?"

*Plain English costs a lot less than legalese*, Raine knew, but he didn't say it out loud.

"It means," he ignored Adam's second, larger question, "that you did something wrong. Something that disqualifies you from a benefit you would otherwise be entitled to."

"Like the company?" Adam asked.

"Like the company," Raine confirmed.

Adam scoffed, a bit too loudly, Raine thought. "What could I possibly have done wrong that would mean I shouldn't inherit my own father's company?"

"Well, see, that goes back to those gifts you mentioned a few minutes ago," Raine answered. He took another, larger sip of the whiskey. There was a chance he might not get to finish the drink if Adam kicked him out of his home after what he was about to suggest. Say. Accuse.

"What are you talking about?" It was as if he didn't even remember saying it.

*Sloppy.* Raine shook his head. And dangerous if he had to take the stand. *When* he had to take the stand.

"The gifts you gave me when the case looked lost," Raine reminded him. Then he went ahead and said it. "Your father's death. And then your brother's death."

Adam squared his shoulders at Raine. "What are you saying?"

"Sit down, Adam," Raine said calmly.

Adam remained standing, fairly menacing over Raine. "I said, wh—"

"And I said," Raine interjected sharply, "*sit down.*"

Adam blinked at him.

That was another thing about being a lawyer. Every interaction was steeped in the psychology of conflict and persuasion. Judges and juries, obviously. Opposing counsel, of course. Lead detectives and injured motorists and lonely widows, yes and yes and yes. But also the clients. Especially the clients. They were hiring you to be a warrior, *their* warrior.

Raine's first boss had told him, "Never negotiate your fee. You're worth what you're worth. If you give an inch to a prospective client, they know you'll cave to the opposition, whether that's a prosecutor or a lawyer for the insurance company or a soon-to-be ex-wife. They know you won't give everything you have to win. They'll think you aren't worth that fee you quoted. And they'll be right."

"There's a reason I came here alone," Raine went on. "A reason we're in your home right now. A reason I didn't bring Rebecca with me, even though she's smart as a whip and would be a witness for me if there was ever any question about what was said between us. That reason is, I need you to understand, completely and fully and instinctively, that anything you say to me right now is absolutely confidential. I am your lawyer. You are my client. Now... Sit. Down."

Adam hesitated, but only for a moment. He returned to his seat across the coffee table from Raine.

"Good," Raine said. "Now tell me how you murdered your father and brother."

## 19

"Did you really say that?" Sommers gasped the next day when Raine recounted his conversation with Adam Harper. "You didn't really say that. Did you?"

They were in Rebecca's office again. The rain was coming down in sheets, pouring down her windows. The sky was dark; it felt like dusk even though it was one o'clock in the afternoon. Raine stood against the wall, arms crossed, watching the water glaze the panes. Sommers was at her desk, leaned back and ready to hear more.

"I did," Raine confirmed.

"And what did he say back?" Sommers asked. "Did he explode? Yell at you? Fire you? What?"

Raine grinned at the memory. "He laughed. He just laughed. A lot. Probably too much. Then he said, 'I like you, Raine. You've got guts. I'll give you that.'"

"Sometimes," Sommers allowed. "Like if there's a dog running at us or something."

"I'd rather fight Adam Harper than a dog," Raine replied. "I could take Adam. Probably. A dog is going to rip my leg to shreds before I can even get a shot in."

Sommers raised an eyebrow at him. "You've actually considered this?"

Raine shrugged. "I guess so. Must be a guy thing."

Sommers shook her head. "Men are weird."

Raine wasn't sure how to argue that point. "Anyway, I pressed the issue. I needed him to tell me the truth. It's not like I can tell anybody anyway. Attorney-client privilege."

"Well, if he did it, don't tell me," Sommers cautioned with a raise of her palm. "I'm not his attorney. I'll call the police and report him before you finish your sentence."

"No, you won't." Raine shook his head. "You work for me, at least on this case. The privilege extends to you too."

"So if one of your clients confesses to murder"— Sommers frowned—"I can't tell the police?"

"Our clients," Raine corrected. "And nope."

Sommers thought for a few moments. "I don't like that."

Raine laughed. "Welcome to the practice of law."

"But I'm not a lawyer," Sommers reminded him. "What would happen if I did tell someone?"

"What would happen if you reported a murder confession to the police in violation of the attorney-client privilege?" Raine confirmed the inquiry. "He'd go to prison for the rest of his life, and I would get disbarred."

Sommers nodded along. "Fine, but what would happen to me?"

Raine thought for a moment. "Well, nothing, I suppose. I mean, your career as a private investigator, such as it is, would be over."

"So I'd have to rely on my award-winning real estate practice?" Sommers smiled and gestured around her well-appointed office.

Raine frowned and crossed his arms a little bit tighter. "You can't tell our clients' secrets. You understand that, right?"

Sommers hesitated, but then threw her hands up. "Fine. I don't like it, but I understand it." She thought for another moment, then added, "Maybe I'm not cut out for this after all. Can't you just have innocent clients? That would make everything a lot easier. For me, anyway."

"Well, that's the goal, obviously," Raine teased. "And I would love it if all my clients were innocent, but then I wouldn't have very many clients."

Sommers allowed a nod to that.

"But don't worry," Raine continued. "Adam did not confess to murdering his father and brother."

"Oh, well, that's a relief." Sommers exhaled. "That's good, right?"

Raine shrugged again. "He didn't deny it explicitly either. He avoided answering the question directly, although the suggestion was that I was crazy for even suspecting him."

"Hm." Sommers raised a hand to her chin.

"Exactly," Raine agreed. "I'd rather he told me the truth, whatever it is. The truth has a way of coming out eventually. I'd like to be prepared for it."

"So, what now?"

Raine pushed himself off the wall and finally took a seat across the desk from his partner. "Now, we get ready for the will contest. Sarah is alleging two things. One, that strict application of the one-hundred-twenty-hour rule would frustrate the true intent of the grantor. And two, that Adam has unclean hands because he maybe, possibly, probably had something to do with his father's and brother's deaths."

"She's actually alleging that?" Sommers asked. "How can she possibly prove it?"

"Well, for one thing," Raine answered, "she can prove it with a lot less evidence than in a criminal case. If Adam were actually charged with the murder, the prosecutor would have to prove it beyond a reasonable doubt. But this is just a will contest. It's civil, not criminal. She would only have to prove it by a preponderance of the evidence. Fifty-one percent."

"I know what a preponderance is," Sommers chastised. "But what evidence does she have?"

"None," Raine answered. "I mean, nothing more than what you and I already suspect. Suspicious timing plus extreme rewards. He went from likely losing everything to owning everything."

"All because of those two deaths." Sommers nodded.

"And she can ask him on the stand," Raine pointed out. "Again, it's not criminal, so he doesn't have the right to remain silent."

"You're going to let him confess to murder on the stand?" Sommers questioned.

"No, of course not. He can always plead the Fifth. But if he does, the judge can use it against him. Again, it's not criminal. If he pulls the same dodgy avoidance he did with me, the judge will know he had something to do with it, and he might lose everything."

Sommers took a deep breath and steepled her hands together. "Would that be so bad? A murderer not benefitting from his murders?"

Raine took a deep breath too. He turned and looked out at the rainy, unnaturally dark afternoon. He found it soothing somehow. "He may be a murderer, but he's my client. So, yes. That would be a bad result."

Sommers shook her head slightly. "I don't know how you do your job sometimes."

Raine laughed darkly. "Me either. Sometimes."

Sommers clasped her hands together. "Okay, well, let's assume Adam is not in fact a murderer and your cause is just."

"It can be just even if he is a murderer," Raine protested, ever the lawyer. "It's about the evidence—"

Sommers raised her hand at him. "Humor me, Dan. As we just discussed, I'm not a lawyer. I'd like to think the man I'm helping is a victim of circumstance, not a cold-blooded killer."

"Fine," Raine allowed.

"So let's assume Adam Harper did not murder half his family," Sommers started.

"More like his entire family," Raine pointed out.

"Even more so, then," Sommers answered. "Let's assume that. That means something else is going on. You just need to figure it out."

"I know that, Rebecca," Raine complained.

"Ah, but do you know how to do it?" Sommers challenged.

Raine sighed. "I mean, not exactly," he admitted.

"Don't underestimate Adam Harper," Sommers warned. "He might not seem like the brightest bulb in the drawer, but he didn't get where he is today just because of who his daddy was. He had the ambition to hire you to take away a multimillion-dollar business, and the confidence to believe he could run it as well or better than the man who founded it. And he's managed to keep you on as his lawyer without giving you the one thing you really want: information."

Raine had to nod along. Adam certainly seemed slow-witted. That didn't mean he was. "So if he won't tell me, how do I find out what really happened?"

"If Adam won't tell you about the mountain," Sommers counseled, "ask the mountain about Adam."

Raine tipped his head to the side at her. "That's not the saying. What are you talking about?"

"There's something about this Harper Tower project that just doesn't add up," Sommers said.

Raine couldn't hardly disagree.

"So if Adam won't tell you about the project from his point of view," Sommers explained, "learn about it from the people on the other side of the project."

"What are you talking about?" Raine asked.

"I'm loath to do this, Dan," she said, "but sometimes things line up in a way that can't be coincidence. You need to find out what's really going on with the Harper Tower, and it just so happens that I'm about to be in a room full of people who might know."

"What people?" Raine asked. "What room?"

Sommers pulled out her phone and pulled up two QR codes. "Two tickets to the annual Greater Seattle Real Estate Agent Association Awards Banquet. Next Friday. And I just lost my planned plus-one."

"Oh really?" Raine raised an eyebrow. "What happened?"

"It turns out his wife has some sort of medical procedure that day."

Raine's eyebrows shot up. "His wife?"

"Yeah, go figure, right?" Sommers sneered. "And no, I didn't know he was married. He told me he was widowed."

"He told you his wife was dead?" Raine scoffed. "What kind of psycho would do that?"

"A very handsome psycho, as it turned out," Sommers admitted. "But once I figured it out, I dumped him. Via text. Group text. Him and his wife."

"Nice," Raine admired.

"Thank you." Sommers smiled. "So you get to be my guest. You will have access to pretty much every high-end real estate agent in the city. There will be plenty of real estate agents who have been involved with the Harper Tower, for better or worse. Do your digging over dinner and champagne."

"And awards," Raine added. "Are you winning any?"

Sommers smiled. "Oh, Dan. Of course I am."

"I will dress accordingly," Raine assured her. "I wouldn't want to take away from your evening. And hopefully I'll learn a thing or two about a thing or two. Too bad it's next Friday, though."

"Why?" Sommers asked.

"Because the first hearing in the will contest is on Monday," Raine answered. "I'll have to do that without knowing whatever your friends are going to tell me."

Sommers leaned forward. "Three things, Dan. One, with some very rare exceptions, they are my colleagues, not my friends. Two, they aren't going to just tell you anything. You're going to have to earn any information you obtain. And three..."

"Yes?" Raine found he really enjoyed talking with Sommers, even on rainy Seattle afternoons. Maybe especially on rainy Seattle afternoons.

"Three," Sommers repeated, "you're going to kill it on Monday."

Raine had told Adam he wasn't his cheerleader. But it was kind of nice to have one of his own.

## 20

Raine didn't see many people before the Monday morning hearing. He'd had his boys for the weekend, which meant he didn't see Sawyer. He didn't want to see Adam. And Rebecca had already given him his pep talk. So it was with extra annoyance that the first person he spoke with that morning was Zac Chapman.

"How was your weekend?" Chapman started the conversation.

Raine was taken aback. They weren't friends. On the contrary, they were, in that very moment, opponents. He expected trash talk, some poor attempt to psych him out, something like that. He didn't have a response ready. But Chapman had his follow-up planned.

"Probably not too exciting, huh?" he said. "You had your boys over the weekend, right? When the kids are with you, you're stuck at home. But if the kids are with your ex, then you can go out on a date. You know what I'm saying?"

Unfortunately, Raine knew exactly what he was saying. But there was no way he was getting dragged into that conversation right then. And not with him. Not until he talked to Natalie first.

Raine pointed at Chapman's smug grin. "You've got some food in your teeth."

It wasn't true, but Chapman covered his mouth—an accomplishment in itself—and turned away to fix his appearance before the judge came out.

Raine turned away as well and stepped over to the table reserved for the defendant. Adam Harper had been the plaintiff when he sued his father. He became a defendant when his brother's widow sued him. And he was already seated at the table, waiting for Raine.

"What was that all about?" he asked.

Raine shook his head. "Nothing. That guy is a jackass, that's all."

"Good," Adam replied.

"Good that he's a jackass?" Raine questioned, and he started unloading his materials from his briefcase to the tabletop.

"Good that you don't like him," Adam clarified. "He clearly doesn't like you either. So it's personal. That's good for me."

"How do you figure?" Raine wasn't going to contest the underlying fact of disliking Chapman.

"Lawyers get paid to argue someone else's case, right?" Adam said. "And that's fine, but you don't really care about the outcome. Professionally, but not personally. Not like I do. Or Sarah does. But if you hate the other lawyer? Now you have your own personal reasons to win. That's perfect. I couldn't have planned it better myself."

Raine paused. Adam Harper seemed like an affable dope. But Sommers had warned him not to underestimate him. Had Adam not only eliminated his father and brother, but also engineered Zac Chapman into being Raine's opposing counsel? Or perhaps he knew Chapman would be his father's lawyer, and that was the reason he'd sought out Raine, because of some half-forgotten, decades-old rivalry. Was Adam really that smart? Raine looked over to Chapman, who, seated next to his client and having likely figured out that he didn't have anything in his teeth after all, returned an icy stare at Raine.

*"Did you plan it?"* Raine considered asking Adam. He wasn't sure he wanted to know the answer. But it was a reminder to take it down a notch, not let it become personal, and win the case based on his professional strengths. Emotion was only going to blur his vision. And he was going to want to see clearly when he stomped his boot into Chapman's face. Figuratively speaking, of course.

Instead, he clapped his client on the back and said, "I'm glad you're happy with the dynamic. I'm looking forward to getting this all behind both of us."

"With a victory," Adam added.

"Yes," Raine confirmed. "With a victory."

They had drawn a different judge than for the original lawsuit. Instead of Judge Malloy, the case had been assigned to Judge Veronica Fairfax. It wasn't a great draw. Prior to being appointed to the bench, she had spent her legal career as an appellate lawyer—the lawyer other lawyers hired to appeal their losses. She was intelligent, detail-oriented, and thorough. She was also exceptionally socially awkward. She had no ability to control the attorneys appearing in front of her, and rulings were always delivered days after the hearing, and in writing, lest she have to speak at length from the bench. It made every hearing feel like an eighth-grade dance where no one had the courage to ask anyone to dance.

She would almost certainly get the correct result, but along the way she would be bowled over by blowhard attorneys, like Chapman, and there was always the risk that she might get herself lost in the deepest of legal weeds, fixated on some piece of minutiae that shouldn't matter, but had been cited one time in a seventy-year-old case that no one but her ever read after it was first published. If there was some ancient, long-forgotten principle of the law that might support Sarah Harper's case, Chapman wouldn't find it, but Fairfax might.

"All rise!" the bailiff bellowed. "The King County Superior Court is now in session, the Honorable Vanessa Fairfax presiding!"

Raine and Adam quickly rose to their feet. Chapman and Sarah did as well. The court reporter remained seated at her machine, and the bailiff was the first one to stand. There was no one else in the courtroom.

Judge Fairfax shuffled out from her chambers. She was a large woman, with thick glasses and dark hair pulled back in a simple ponytail. She avoided eye contact with any of those assembled in her courtroom and moved directly to take her perch atop the bench. "You may be seated," she instructed quietly.

Raine and Adam sat down as directed, but Chapman remained standing. His client wavered, looking from her lawyer to the judge, then sat down uncertainly.

"Thank you and good morning, Your Honor," Chapman belted out. "This is the matter of Sarah Harper versus Adam Harper ex rel. the Estate of William Harper. I am Zachary

Chapman, and I am proud to appear on behalf of the plaintiff, Sarah Harper."

Judge Fairfax stared down at Chapman for several seconds. "Um, thank you, counsel. You can be seated now."

She was a kind and patient person, not always common among judges. Raine's plan was to appeal to those qualities. Chapman's appeared to be to try to take advantage of them.

"If I might, Your Honor." Chapman did not sit down. "I'd like to lay out the issues in this litigation so the Court might better understand the questions presented and more readily arrive at the just result."

Judge Fairfax was also very likely the smartest person in the room, literally. It was the one thing she seemed comfortable about. Raine smiled slightly as Chapman suggested the judge might have trouble understanding anything, let alone his legal strategy.

"That won't be necessary, counsel," the judge replied, still declining to use Chapman's name. "I have read the initial pleadings, and I am very familiar with the law surrounding the issues presented by your complaint."

"Ah, see, that's just it." Chapman raised a finger into the air. "The Court may be familiar with the settled law in this area, but we are asking the Court to expand on the existing law, extend it, improve it. It is this aspect of our suit that I would like to address at the outset."

Judge Fairfax frowned, and not subtly. She wasn't known for being good at reading other people's emotions naturally, and she made little effort to conceal her own.

"I don't think that will be necessary, Mr. Chapman," she repeated. Then, giving ground, she turned to Raine. "Unless Mr. Raine would like to also deliver some sort of opening remarks this morning. If either lawyer feels the need to put on some sort of show for their client, then I suppose I could endure that before we get to the actual purposes of this morning's hearing."

Raine smiled more broadly. He hadn't appeared very many times in front of Judge Fairfax, and then only for brief, onetime hearings. He thought he was going to enjoy doing an entire trial in front of her.

He stood up to answer the judge. "No, thank you, Your Honor," he said. "I prefer to give my opening statements to the jury. And I feel no need to put on a show for Mr. Harper in order to justify my fee."

He stole a sidelong glance at Chapman and was gratified to see him stewing, fists clenched. Judges weren't supposed to expose lawyers' business tricks. Raine had the advantage that whatever Adam already thought of him, it wasn't going to change from a five-minute speech.

"I would prefer," Raine continued, "that we move directly to the issue of scheduling. I'm sure we will have more than enough opportunity to present our arguments to the Court when the time is appropriate."

Judge Fairfax nodded. "I agree, Mr. Raine. This is not the time. I think it's important that we do things at the appropriate time. Otherwise, things could get out of control very quickly, and I don't like it when things get out of control." She looked again at Chapman.

Chapman just stood there and stared back at the judge.

"You may sit down now, Mr. Chapman," she instructed for the third time.

Chapman finally complied, and Raine followed suit before the judge even needed to ask him.

"Now then." Judge Fairfax cleared her throat, a louder and more unpleasant sound than Raine might have anticipated. "I like to work backwards. We will schedule a trial date first, then fill in dates for any pretrial hearings. This will be a bench trial, so I would propose a trial date in two months."

Chapman jumped to his feet again. "I'm not sure the plaintiff can be ready that quickly, Your Honor. We were going to propose a trial date in early next year. Also, we will be asking for a jury."

"I would have thought the parties would want a speedy resolution to this litigation," Judge Fairfax responded. "The control of a very large corporation is at stake, and it is my understanding that there is a rather substantial construction project being held up by the uncertainty in ownership of that company. Why would you want to wait until next year to resolve this?"

Chapman displayed that smug grin of his again. Raine had hated it back in law school and hated it then, years later. Fortunately, the judge didn't seem too fond of it either.

"Well, Your Honor, that was part of why I wished to address the Court at the outset," he complained. "We will be asking the Court to grant a preliminary injunction preventing either party from taking any action that significantly affects the assets of the corporation, then establish a receivership for the Court to authorize the continuing payment of workers and contractors attached to the Harper Tower project so that the building can be completed while this litigation unfolds."

Adam grabbed Raine's arm. "No!" he only half whispered. "That's not acceptable. This is my company, and I need to be able to do whatever I want with it. We need this resolved as soon as possible, not next year."

Raine extracted his arm from his client's grasp and

patted his hand. "I understand," he assured him, his own voice lowered. He just didn't fully understand why. But that didn't matter right then.

"What is your response to all of that, Mr. Raine?" the judge invited. "And to the request for a jury. Generally speaking, will contests are tried to a judge, not a jury."

"I want a jury too." Adam grabbed Raine's arm again. "I'll do great with a jury. People like me."

Raine had his doubts about that. And about trying the case to a jury. There was an old saying among criminal defense attorneys: if you're guilty, try your case to a jury; if you're innocent, try your case to a judge. Raine had the black-letter law on his side. He would rather have a judge follow the law than risk a jury following their hearts. On the other hand, there was a way to take two bites of the apple.

"We have no objection to a jury, Your Honor." Raine answered the second question first. "Although this action is mostly a will contest, the plaintiff has also asserted certain bad acts by my client that exceed the usual attack on the four corners of a will. There is a basis to extend the use of a jury to this case, and we will not object to that."

Fairfax frowned, but nodded.

"However, as to the proposals of a preliminary injunction to freeze the company and setting a trial date next year, we are very much opposed to both of those. We agree with the Court that this matter can and should be ready for trial in two months. Furthermore, we would suggest scheduling a hearing on our motion to dismiss in one week's time." He pulled a pleading off the top of the documents he had unloaded onto the table. He stepped over to deliver a copy to Chapman and the original to the bailiff. "The plaintiff's lawsuit is contrary to all existing law in this field. I think the case can be disposed of expeditiously."

"One week?" It was Chapman's turn to complain out of turn.

"The court rules only require five working days' notice," Raine reminded him.

"Please address any comments to the bench," Judge Fairfax scolded, "not to each other. But Mr. Raine is correct. Five working days' notice is the minimum required. Do you want more time to respond, Mr. Chapman? I am willing to schedule the hearing in two weeks rather than one if you need additional time."

The truth was, everything a lawyer did in open court was a show for their client. Chapman had to choose between being prepared or appearing confident. "One week will be fine, Your Honor."

"Good." Fairfax nodded. "You will file any response to the defendant's motion no later than this Thursday. Mr. Raine, any reply is due by the end of business Friday. We will reconvene next Monday morning for argument on the defendant's motion to dismiss."

"Shall we discuss further scheduling this morning?" Chapman suggested. "And the plaintiff's motion for a preliminary injunction?"

Judge Fairfax smiled down at him. "Why don't we resolve the motion to dismiss first? The resolution of that may obviate the need for any further decisions by the Court."

Raine liked the sound of that. Adam did too. He shook Raine's hand vigorously. "Great job," he whispered.

Raine demurred. "Let's wait for the hearing. We haven't won anything yet."

"With that," Judge Fairfax said, "court is adjourned."

"All rise!" the bailiff called out again, and everyone stood while the judge disappeared to her chambers.

Raine assessed the room. He was pleased. Adam was happy. Chapman was angry. And Sarah seemed concerned.

*Perfect.*

## 21

The award banquet for the Greater Seattle Real Estate Agent Association was being held at the Mercer Club, a banquet facility to the north of downtown, between the hip Belltown District and the freeways that separated downtown from the even hipper Capitol Hill neighborhood.

The club shared its name with several other landmarks in the area. There was a Mercer Street, a Mercer Arena, even a city and actual island in Lake Washington named Mercer Island, the city's most expensive suburb. Asa Mercer had been one of the city's founders and led a trip back to the Eastern United States to recruit women willing to marry the mostly male population of what was then a frontier outpost on the North Pacific. The mission had been a success and cemented Asa Mercer's legacy. There had even been a TV show about it back in the 1960s. Raine always found the story a bit strange, but he supposed times were different back then. Either way, it was the only thing he, or most Seattleites, remembered about any of the city's early founders.

The building itself was a squat structure, surrounded mostly by parking lots and other squat buildings. At one time it had probably been prime real estate, but the waves of gentrification had swept to either side of the area, leaving the luxury venue high and dry. Raine appreciated the irony of a real estate award banquet being held in that particular part of the city. At least there was plenty of parking.

Once he was inside, Raine understood why they had chosen the venue. Luxuriously appointed, the outside world of freeways and parking lots melted away into a grand hall from yesteryear. At least the foyer was grand, decorated in velvet and gold leaf.

The event was advertised to begin at 6:00 p.m., and while Raine wasn't always the most punctual person, he could make extra efforts when the occasion called for it. He arrived some ten minutes late for the purported start of the event, but found himself to be the first person to arrive, which was even more awkward because he wasn't on the guest list. He was someone else's plus-one, so he had to wait in the lobby for another twenty minutes before Sommers finally arrived. But when he saw her, he smiled. At least he had managed to dress appropriately.

Sommers was wearing a silk champagne-colored dress that ended just above the knee. Her throat and wrists were covered in pearls and gold, and her long platinum hair cascaded in loose waves down her bare back. Three-inch white stilettos completed the look.

Raine had chosen a black suit, a white shirt, and in a moment of reckless abandon, a pale pink floral tie, rather than red stripes. Men had it easier.

"You look nice," Sommers approved upon seeing him in the lobby.

"And you look like someone who's going to win an award tonight." Raine returned the compliment. "Maybe two."

"Definitely two," Sommers replied with a grin. "Did you wait out here just for me? You should have gone in and started mingling."

Raine shrugged. "Well, first, there was no one else here when I got here. And second, they wouldn't let me in without my date."

Sommers grimaced at the last word of his sentence. "Let's avoid the d-word," she instructed. "You're my plus-one, but you're not who I'm going home with tonight."

"Oh really?" Raine raised a curious eyebrow. "And who are you going home with tonight?"

Sommers grinned again and nodded toward the entrance to the gala. "Let's go inside and find out."

———

IT DIDN'T TAKE LONG for the venue to fill up. No one wanted to be the first to arrive, but by the looks of it, no one wanted to miss the event either. Soon enough, the ballroom was wall to wall with attendees. Music and conversation filled the hall, and Raine suddenly wished he could have brought Sawyer. But plus-ones don't get to bring their own plus-ones.

"Do you know everyone here?" Raine asked Sommers after they had gotten their first round of drinks from the open bar.

Sommers took a sip of her gin and tonic and surveyed the room. "I do. Except for a few of the dates, but even most of them I know. That's how you get ahead in this business. You know people."

"Connections." Raine nodded knowingly.

"More than connections," Sommers answered. "You have connections. You know other lawyers. Maybe some judges, like your old law partner. If you need something, maybe you know who to call for a referral. But knowing people, that takes more. That takes time. That takes skill."

"Well, do you know anyone who might have some information about my case?" Raine gestured toward the crowd with his old-fashioned. "Who should we talk to first?"

"We aren't going to talk to anyone, dear friend," Sommers answered. "I am going to introduce you to a few select people who might have some information about the Harper Tower or Harper Development or the Harper family generally. I am not going to mention anything about that at all. Then I am going to make an excuse to leave, and you will have to use your own skills to extract whatever information you can."

Raine frowned. "Why are we doing it that way? Won't they be more likely to talk to you? They will have just met me."

"I am not burning any of my carefully curated connections for your case," Sommers answered. "Don't get me wrong. I want you to succeed. I want to help. I wouldn't have brought you here if I didn't. But if people think I brought you here to interrogate them, with my knowledge, well, that's the sort of thing that damages relationships. That turns them into just connections."

Raine nodded. "That's very... self-protective of you."

"If I don't protect myself, no one will," she answered.

Raine wasn't sure that was exactly true, but he understood her point. And he wasn't going to begrudge her for protecting her own career ahead of his. She was still helping him. "So, who do I talk to first?"

"There are three people I think are worth talking to tonight," Sommers said. She pointed into the crowd, as if Raine would have any idea who any of the names she was about to recite belonged to. "Deborah Yao. Ethan Fassbinder. And Emily Park."

Raine made a mental note of each name, in the event he and Sommers got separated and he had to track them down on his own somehow.

"Deborah," Sommers explained, "owns one of the most prestigious brokerages in the city. She sells the top properties to the top people, and she does it before anyone else even knows the property is going to be on the market. Ethan just set up his own agency, but before that he worked for Essex Realty. The owners of that, Andrew and Audrey Essex, were good friends with Bill Harper. I think Andrew and Bill were on the rowing team in college together."

"What about Emily Park?" Raine asked.

Sommers chuckled. "Emily just knows everything about everybody, especially the shady stuff. If you don't get anything from Deborah or Ethan, you'll definitely get something from Emily. It may not help your case, but it'll be entertaining."

"And what are you going to be doing?" Raine asked.

"My job, Dan." She patted him on the cheek, her tangle of bracelets jangling in his ear. "My job."

Deborah Yao was on the far side of the ballroom, but that was fine with Raine. It gave him a chance to people-gawk as they traversed a room full of professionals who took meticulous care of their appearance. They knew that clients expected them to look rich, because rich meant successful, and successful meant good. The same logic should have applied to lawyers, but the law was a profession at least half-filled with misfits. The people who couldn't think of anything better to do for a living, but definitely wanted to avoid math and/or heavy lifting. The legal profession had one of the highest rates of substance abuse and suicide. There were plenty of lawyers who were lucky to pull on a suit and find a courthouse on any given day.

"Deborah!" Sommers called out as they reached Raine's first target. "How are you? You look amazing tonight. Of course! Just like every night."

Sommers and Yao exchanged kisses on the cheek, and Yao complimented Sommers's appearance in return. Yao was average height, with short black hair, a simple single gold necklace, and a sleeveless blue dress that ended mid-calf. Raine guessed her age at about fifty-five.

"Please allow me to introduce you to my companion for the evening." Sommers gestured to Raine. "This is Daniel Raine. He's a local attorney whom I've sort of adopted."

Adopted? Raine cocked his head slightly at Sommers.

"When my plus-one had to cancel on me, I decided to let him see how real professionals celebrate our accomplishments," Sommers continued. "I just hope he doesn't embarrass me."

Deborah Yao smiled at Raine and extended a hand in greeting. "It's a pleasure to meet you, Mr. Raine."

Raine shook the offered hand. "Pleasure to meet you as well, Ms. Yao. And please, call me Dan."

"Deborah." She returned the offer of familiarity. "So, what kind of law do you practice? Real estate? Is that how you met Rebecca?"

"I'm kind of a jack-of-all-trades," Raine answered. "I do whatever comes in the door. Mostly courtroom stuff.

Lawsuits, wills, even some criminal defense if I can't avoid it."

"Lovely," Deborah said in a way that made clear she didn't think it was lovely at all.

"And how did you meet Rebecca, then?" Deborah asked. "Unless she has some sordid crime drama story we don't know about yet."

"You know all of my sordid stories." Sommers laughed. "No, I met Dan when I was going to sell his office out from under him. But I liked him, so instead I helped him solve a case or two along the way."

Deborah offered a surprised smile. "Is that right, Dan?"

Raine took a moment to answer. He didn't like how Sommers had phrased it, but he didn't suppose he was going to be very successful with Deborah Yao if he started their interaction with an argument with Sommers.

Fortunately, Sommers bailed him out. "I may have exaggerated a bit," she conceded, "but we have had occasion to consult each other when the need arose. Sometimes Dan's practice does brush up against what we do. Why, he's currently representing Adam Harper, aren't you, Dan?"

Raine was surprised Sommers went so far as to tell Deborah that. He thought he was on his own. But then, after a moment, he was.

"But I will let him tell you about that," Sommers said, craning her neck to look somewhere in the crowd. "I see someone I absolutely must say hello to. It was wonderful to see you, Deborah."

"You as well, Rebecca," Deborah agreed, and they parted after another exchange of cheek kisses.

Deborah's smile faded as Sommers receded into the

crowd; then she turned and looked directly into Raine's eyes. "What do you want to know about Adam Harper?"

Raine was taken aback. He didn't expect Deborah to be so direct or Sommers to be so wrong. And he wasn't sure how to answer the question.

"Uh, well, that is," he stammered. "I mean, anything you might know about him would be of interest to me, of course. I'm his lawyer, so, um, yeah. What can you tell me?"

"I could tell you a lot," Deborah answered. "But how about we start with you telling me something I want to know."

"Okay," Raine agreed. Then, because of that whole pesky attorney-client privilege, he added, "If I can."

Deborah sighed. "Of course. Well, tell me this, Daniel Raine. When is that Harper Tower project going to get back up and running? I have several clients waiting to move in there when construction is complete, but they can't wait forever. How long will this delay be?"

Raine took a deep breath and nodded. He was permitted to tell her anything she could find out by going down to the courthouse and looking at the public case file. "I don't know." He could also tell her that. It didn't violate any attorney-client confidences. And it was true. "The entire company is caught up in litigation about who should rightfully control the business."

"Bill Harper should still be controlling the business," Deborah said. "But that isn't possible anymore, so I just want someone who will get things back on track so my clients don't lose their deposits."

"Why would they lose their deposits?" Raine asked.

Deborah smiled at him. "You really don't do real estate law, do you?"

Raine shook his head.

"The deposits secure the units once construction is done," Deborah explained. "If Harper Tower doesn't get back on track soon, some of my clients may have to walk away from their deposits and look elsewhere."

"They can't just wait until it's finished?" Raine wondered.

"Some of them probably can," Deborah answered, "but these are residential units. My clients want somewhere to live. If they can't move into their Harper Tower unit in the time they expected, they might be forced to find another place to call home."

"Can they get a refund?"

"Generally speaking, deposits are nonrefundable. Small delays are to be expected in any project like this, so Harper expressly excluded construction delays as a reason for deposit refunds. The only way to get a refund would be if the tower is never finished, and the city won't let that happen. They'll force construction to finish, even if that means Harper Development has to sell the project to another developer. Harper would only do that if they went bankrupt, and if they're bankrupt—"

"They can't refund the deposits anyway," Raine realized.

"Exactly." Deborah pointed a finger at him. "Can you help me? Can you get that project back on track?"

"I'm trying." Raine felt like he could tell her that too. "I have a motion to dismiss scheduled for this Monday. It's what we call a 12(b)(6) motion and—"

"Oh, no!" Deborah interrupted and raised a hand to his face. "Do not start citing the law to me. Nothing will destroy a festive mood faster than a lawyer talking about the law."

Raine had to admit that he was about to be very technical and boring.

"You just get that project back on track, Dan." Deborah pointed at him again. "I have a dozen clients who are counting on it." With that, she took her leave, albeit without any kisses, on the cheek or otherwise.

Raine watched her melt into the crowd, largely because he wasn't sure what else to do. Sommers was nowhere to be seen. He also still had most of his drink left, so he couldn't really justify another trip to the bar. Not yet, anyway. He supposed he could just mingle with no ulterior motives, asking people about their latest real estate transaction, where they got their outfit from, maybe something about the weather. That sounded terrible, but most of what he did was terrible. He took a large swig of his old-fashioned and waded into the crowd.

Mercifully, it only took three explanations of a purchase-and-sale agreement, two war stories about crazy clients, and one "I'm sorry. I'm only here to talk to other real estate agents," for Raine to stumble across Sommers again. She was engaged in what appeared to be a hilarious conversation about some aspect of her work that he knew nothing about. He could have stepped up and stood awkwardly next to her until the laughter stopped and people were no longer enjoying the conversation. Or he could, as he instead chose to do, step a few feet away, keep an eye on Sommers, and descend upon her when she broke off from the group. It took about five or six minutes, but eventually, Sommers was free again, and Raine reached out for her.

"Oh, hey there, stranger," Sommers greeted him. "How did your conversation with Deborah go?"

"Pretty well," Raine appraised. "I learned that there are dozens of potential buyers who may lose their deposits if the Harper Tower project doesn't get back on track soon."

"Hmm." Sommers raised a hand to her chin. "What do you think that might mean?"

"Well, it might be a reason to keep stalling the project," Raine suggested. "Then Adam could just pocket the deposit money."

Sommers shook her head. "There is so much more money to be made by finishing that building A.S.A.P. and selling all of the units."

Raine supposed that was probably true.

"And isn't it Sarah who wants to delay everything?" Sommers asked. "Your guy wants a quick dismissal and the keys to the company, right?"

That was also true. To a degree.

"He wants the company right away," Raine agreed, "but I'm not sure if he wants to get the tower back on track. Even before Chapman filed the lawsuit, things had ground to a halt because he wasn't paying vendors."

Sommers squinted at Raine. "Who's Chapman?"

Raine sighed. "Zac Chapman. He's my opposing counsel. Nothing more."

Sommers pursed her lips and nodded. "The way you said all of that tells me he is clearly more than just your opposing counsel."

"I don't want to talk about it." Raine waved the subject away. "Let's get back to our plan. Who's next? Ethan somebody, right?"

"Ethan Fassbinder, yes," Sommers confirmed. She raised her gaze and scanned the ballroom. "There he is! Come on, let's go before someone else grabs him."

"He's that interesting?" Raine asked.

"He's that hot," Sommers answered.

"Beating the ladies off with a stick, huh?" Raine invoked the old saw.

Sommers smiled. "I'm pretty sure he takes all comers. But yeah, he's very popular and will only become more so as the bar gets drained. Come on."

Sommers grabbed Raine's hand and pulled him quickly through the crowd, bouncing him off more than one annoyed reveler. He mumbled apologies as he worked to extract his hand from Sommers's grip, but her grasp was surprisingly strong. By the time he managed to extract his hand, it was because she had let go. They had reached Ethan Fassbinder. And he was gorgeous.

Tall, athletic, stylish, with the face of an angel. A hot angel. Sandy blond hair swept away from his perfect features and sparkling eyes. He was laughing at something the man next to him had said, which showcased his bright white teeth and a dimple on only one side of his mouth. Even the asymmetry was perfect. And the laugh was deep, but warm, inviting. Raine could see why Sommers had wanted to hurry. There was an actual line forming to speak with him. Or maybe just to stand in front of him and bathe in his radiance.

Sommers wasn't one to wait in lines. "Ethan!" she called out as she stepped in to give him a hug. He hugged her back gladly. She had her own high level of radiance.

"Rebecca! I was so hoping I would see you tonight," he said when they separated again. "You're a shoo-in for that commercial real estate agent of the year award."

Sommers waved a hand at the suggestion. "I'm just here to see old friends and make new ones. If I win an award or two while I'm here, that's icing on the cake."

"Or two!" Ethan laughed. "Oh, Rebecca, you are too much. Now I hope you win three."

Raine was starting to think being part of the socially impaired legal profession was maybe not so bad after all. Not that he had any problem with how Sommers, and everyone else for that matter, was working the room. It just looked exhausting. He had a finite amount of social energy, and when it was gone, he would be happy to sit on a bar stool in mutually agreed silence with a chemically dependent fellow member of the bar.

"I'll try to leave some awards for you, Ethan dear." Rebecca slapped a playful hand on his muscular chest. "In the meantime, I'd like to introduce you to my plus-one this evening. This is Daniel Raine. He's an attorney, but try not to hold that against him."

Raine smiled weakly at yet another lawyer joke and extended a hand. "Nice to meet you, Ethan."

Ethan's grip was strong without being crushing, warm without being clammy. Raine enjoyed the sensation of touching him. He found it unsettling.

"Ethan just set up his own real estate agency." Sommers pretended not to have already told Raine. "Dan is also a solo practitioner. He owns his own firm. I mean, since his law partner abandoned him."

Raine forced a smile at that last bit. "Thanks, Rebecca." Then, to Ethan, "I'm sure running a real estate agency is a lot different from running a law firm. How long have you been out on your own?"

"Oh!" Sommers interjected. She reached out and laid a hand on Ethan's arm. "I'm sorry, but I need to step away for a moment. I just saw someone I have been trying to track down for ages. Can I leave Dan in your capable hands?"

Ethan smiled, first at Sommers, then at Raine, then again at Sommers. "Oh, yes."

Raine wasn't sure he liked the unspoken messages between them, but he had endured worse in his career. Occasional humiliation was part of representing people who had screwed up enough to need a lawyer and were dumb enough to lie to them. Like Adam Harper.

Sommers departed, and Ethan turned his attention back to Raine. "I'm sorry, did you just ask me a question?"

"I did," Raine confirmed. "I asked how long you've been out on your own."

"Ah, yes." Ethan smiled warmly at him. "Only a few months now. I worked at Essex Realty for, well, I'd better not say, lest I give away my age."

Raine had originally estimated Ethan's age as mid-thirties, but that comment made him wonder if he might be more like forty, with some work done.

"Essex?" Raine feigned ignorance. "Is that a big agency?"

"Oh, yes." Ethan nodded strongly. "One of the biggest."

Raine frowned slightly. "I don't think I've ever seen their signs around. Do they do residential?"

"You wouldn't see their signs." Ethan chuckled. "We sold homes that never went to market. Private purchases, arranged in advance, all very high value, and clients who preferred to stay out of public sight and certainly weren't about to get into some pedestrian bidding war for a property they wanted."

"Wow." Raine nodded along. "Sounds lucrative."

"Oh, it was," Ethan confirmed. He took a sip of his drink. "Very lucrative."

"So why did you leave?" Raine asked the obvious question. And the one that would lead to further questions whose answers he actually cared about.

Ethan paused before answering, his strong mouth twisted into a thoughtful knot. "It was just time for me to go. Don't get me wrong. The Essexes treated me very well. Almost like a son. Almost. But even a child has to strike out on his own eventually. I guess there just wasn't room for me there anymore."

Raine again nodded along to Ethan's answer. There was a lot more behind each of those sentences. Especially the repeated and singular "almost".

"Even real families can start to feel too small," Raine offered. "I have a client who may have stayed too long in the family firm. Now it's starting to unravel around him."

Ethan twisted that knot in his mouth a bit tighter. "Would that family firm happen to be in the real estate development industry?"

Raine smiled, but demurred. "That would be saying too much, I think. Attorney-client privilege and all."

"That's not a no," Ethan pointed out.

"That's not a no," Raine confirmed. "Are you familiar with that particular family?"

"The one you can't name?"

"That one precisely," Raine answered. "I mean, you could certainly name them. You're not their attorney. And if you happen to know anything that might be helpful to another solo businessman just trying to make rent, well, I would be very grateful."

Ethan raised an eyebrow at him. "How grateful?"

Raine was pretty sure they were flirting, but he didn't have any precedential experience to draw on for confirmation. Still, it seemed to be working. "I suppose it might depend on how valuable the information is, and whether it helps or hurts my client. If you had any dirt on my unnamed client's unnamed father, that could be useful. Very useful."

Ethan sighed out through his nose and glanced around their immediate surroundings. He poured what was left of his drink down his throat and motioned for Raine to step in closer. Raine complied, and Ethan put an arm around him. They were roughly the same height—Ethan might have been an inch taller—so his arm rested naturally over Raine's shoulders.

"Bill Harper was a mean old son of a bitch," Ethan whispered into his ear, "and he learned it from Andy Essex."

"Really?" Raine whispered back, a bit awkwardly given their relative positions.

"Really," Ethan answered. "In fact, it was Andy who told Bill to change his will after Adam sued him. I mean, if you know anything about that," he added with a laugh.

"I might." Raine returned the chuckle. "But why?"

"They went way back," Ethan explained. "College. Maybe even high school. They're both ruthless businessmen who fought to the tops of their professions. And they helped each other out along the way. You don't sell high-end properties before they go to market without having a connection to the main guy building those high-end properties. And you don't build those properties without having a connection to the main guy selling them for you."

"That makes a lot of sense," Raine said. He wondered when Ethan might take his arm off him. Not yet, apparently.

"I can tell you this much, Dan." He leaned in even closer, his lips brushing Raine's ear. "They were birds of a feather. Tough, mean, ruthless birds of a heartless feather. We live in a society where sociopaths go to jail, unless they go into business, in which case they go straight to the top."

"Are you saying Bill Harper and Andy Essex were both sociopaths?" That would be something to confirm somehow.

Ethan suddenly yanked his arm away from Raine and stood up strangely straight. "I think what I'm saying is too much." He shook his head, looked at his empty glass, then shook his head again. "It was nice to meet you, Mr. Raine. I think we should both try to forget this conversation."

Fat chance, Raine thought, even as he said, "Good idea. It was nice to meet you too, Ethan."

But Ethan Fassbinder already had his back to Raine, hurrying to return to his line of adorers.

Raine looked at his own glass and decided not to drink any further from it until he'd had some food. He didn't want to say anything he might regret himself. It was time to find Rebecca again.

It was easier to interrupt her this time. She was in a semicircle of people, nodding along to something someone else was saying. No one was laughing or really seemed entertained to any appreciable degree. Sommers seemed relieved to have a reason to excuse herself when Raine arrived.

"How did that go?" she asked once they stepped away from the crowd a bit.

"I think he hit on me," Raine started.

Sommers nodded. "Probably. You look good tonight."

Raine grinned down at himself. "Really?"

"Focus, Dan." Sommers shook her head at him. "Did you learn anything?"

"I think there was a lot more to learn," Raine answered, "but he kind of freaked out when he called his old boss a sociopath and broke off the conversation."

"A sociopath? Andrew Essex?" Sommers laughed at first, but then thought about it for a moment. "Yeah, I could see that, actually. It could be an asset in this line of work. Seeing people as a means to make money rather than actual human beings."

"They can be both," Raine suggested. It wasn't like he didn't make money off of other people's misery himself.

"Of course they can." Sommers patted his cheek again. He was going to have to ask her to stop doing that at some point. "Anything else?"

Raine considered. "Maybe. I think I need some time to decipher what he was saying between the lines."

Sommers gazed over the crowd. "I haven't seen Emily Park yet, but they're about to serve dinner anyway. That will give you time to decipher whatever you'd like."

Raine held up his booze glass. "And get something in our stomachs."

"Yes, that too," Sommers agreed. "You always want to let the other person be the one who says something they regret."

———

DINNER WAS in an adjoining room filled with round, white-tableclothed tables, each seating eight guests comfortably. Unfortunately, they sat ten to a table, and the result was anything but comfortable. Raine had to press his elbows into his sides as he cut his chicken cordon blue, and the only place he could find to set his drink was too far to reach after he'd sat down. Sommers was on one side of him, but she spent most of the dinner talking to the person on her other side. The woman on Raine's other side was likewise continually engaged with the colleague to her other side. Raine was left to eat his dinner quietly, alone in a crowded room. At least the food was good, and the waitstaff brought extra rolls. It could have been worse.

The awards ceremony followed directly after dinner. Everyone made their way back into the ballroom to the clinking of the waitstaff bussing the tables behind them. While everyone was eating dinner, the ballroom had been transformed from an empty room with a bar in the back, to a room filled with an awards table and speaker's podium, rows of folding chairs, and still a bar in the back.

Sommers grabbed two seats in the front row while Raine went to get them fresh drinks. The line was longer than he would have liked, and by the time he returned to their seats, the first speaker was starting his welcome remarks.

"Here you go." Raine extended Sommers's drink to her.

But she shushed him and waved the drink away. She was focused intently on the speaker.

Raine sighed and tried to count the number of awards sitting on the table, waiting to be given away. He stopped counting after twenty. It was going to be a long night.

## 22

The Greater Seattle Real Estate Agent Association gave away twenty-seven awards that night. Sommers won two of them.

She was ecstatic. Raine was ready to go home. They never did find Emily Park.

"I'm sorry you didn't get to talk to more people," Sommers offered as they made their way to the exit. She held up her pair of crystal sculptures. "But the night wasn't a total loss."

"The night was an absolute success!" Raine offered her a small clap, to which she responded with a curtsey.

He would have liked to have gotten more information on the Harpers, but he wasn't about to rain on Sommers's parade. The Seattle sky, on the other hand, had no such reservations. A misty rain greeted the departing guests. And neither of them had remembered to bring a coat, just in case.

Raine quickly pulled off his suit jacket and held it over Sommers's head. "Here, I'll walk you to your car."

"Oh, Dan, you don't have to do that," Sommers protested. "I won't melt."

"That dress might," Raine pointed out. "I don't think silk is supposed to get rained on."

Sommers looked at her gown and acquiesced. "Okay. Thanks."

"Where are you parked?" Raine asked. Just because he was being gallant didn't mean they couldn't hurry. The rain was already picking up. It stung his face, and he could feel the back of his shoulders getting wet already.

"Around the block," Sommers answered.

"Come on," he said. "Let's cut through the alley."

Sommers hesitated.

"It's okay." Raine answered her unspoken question. "We're far enough away from Third Avenue and not close enough to the freeway overpasses. There shouldn't be any homeless people in there. Just garbage dumpsters and quickly growing puddles. You probably don't want to get your shoes wet either, so watch your step."

They hurried along the sidewalk as best they could among the other departing guests, who were also trying to figure out the best way to avoid the rain descending upon them. Sommers had taken over holding up one half of the jacket. Raine held up the other and steered Sommers into the alleyway with his other hand. They were making good time and avoiding the puddles.

It wasn't until they were passing the dumpster behind the back exit of the award venue that they were stopped dead in their tracks by the sudden appearance of Ethan Fassbinder, looming large in the increasing downpour and disturbingly unconcerned by the rain drenching him.

"Raine!" he yelled. At first, it wasn't clear if he meant the weather or the man in front of him, but then he added, "Dan Raine! That's your name, right?"

He was drunk. Very drunk. And a man that size needed a lot to get that drunk.

"Hey there, Ethan," Raine answered, trying to sound casual despite the circumstances. "Fun night, huh? We're just trying to get to our car, so if you could—"

"Fun night?" he yelled, stumbling a step to his left from the force of his own voice. "You think it was a fun night?"

Raine looked at Sommers, who slightly raised the two awards tucked under her arm.

"I had fun," Sommers said.

"I wanted to have fun!" Ethan shouted. "I was going to have fun despite everything. But you ruined it, Raine. You ruined everything."

Again, there was some ambiguity about what had ruined Ethan's evening. Raine pointed to his chest. "Me?"

"Yes, you!" That clarified it. "Who the hell are you anyway? Some damn lawyer coming to a real estate award banquet? What kind of bullshit is that? And then you come up to me and start asking about my boss and why he fired me. Who the hell do you think you are?"

"You were fired?" Sommers gasped. "I thought you chose to go out on your own."

"Why would I ever do that?" Ethan grabbed his head with both hands. "Do you know what I was making there? Do you know how hard it is to run your own agency?"

"I mean, yeah." Sommers nodded at her awards. "That's what one of these was for. Best Solo Commercial Real Estate Agent."

"Shut up!" Ethan cried out. He pointed at Raine. "He fired me because of you! Because of your client!"

"Because of Adam Harper?" Raine asked, increasingly dumbfounded.

"Oh, so you can say his name." Ethan shook his head violently. "More lies. It was all lies, wasn't it? You and that bastard Adam Harper. Andy took one look at what his best friend's son did to him, and he never trusted me again. I wasn't even his real son. He realized I could try to do the same thing, call him senile and try to steal the business from him. Bill told him to fire me, and he did. All because of you!"

"Well, I mean that's really more on Adam, I think," Raine replied. "And Bill. And Andy. Not me."

"Definitely not you," Sommers agreed.

Ethan charged Raine, and before Raine could react, Ethan tackled him. They crashed to the ground, Ethan's massive body crushing Raine into the wet pavement. Luckily, the impact twisted their relative positions enough to free up one of Raine's arms. Ethan was larger, younger, and undoubtedly stronger. But Raine was sober, which meant he should be quicker. He drove his free elbow into the back of Ethan's head, sending his face into the pavement. Ethan's grip on Raine relaxed temporarily, and Raine pulled himself from underneath his attacker. He pushed himself to his feet and squared off against Ethan, who was already standing up as well, his nose bleeding from its impact with the street.

"We don't need to do this," Raine tried.

But Ethan was beyond talking to. He raised his fists as well and began stepping toward Raine, looking for an opening.

"Stop!" Sommers screamed. "Both of you! Just stop!"

Raine wasn't about to stop if Ethan didn't. He didn't bother responding to Sommers's entreaty. He needed to focus on Ethan's actions, not Sommers's words.

Ethan took a couple of jabbing steps at Raine, testing his defenses, then stepped in to throw a full punch with all of his weight. Raine managed to raise an arm, but the swing was strong enough to connect anyway, albeit with less force than intended. That was good because, even at a reduced velocity, Ethan's fist crashed into Raine's cheek and sent him reeling backward into the brick wall behind him. Ethan advanced and followed with a blow to Raine's stomach, doubling him over. Even drunk, Ethan was plenty quick.

Raine countered with a punch to Ethan's gut that had marginal effect. Another toward Ethan's face that glanced off his ear. And another that managed to connect on Ethan's already injured nose.

Ethan stumbled backward, covering his face in pain. Raine jumped forward and threw another punch at Ethan's head, but most of it struck Ethan's already raised arms, so Raine turned and kicked Ethan in the stomach, sending him backward again and into the wooden fence on the other side of the alleyway. Raine felt like he might be turning the tide. He was wrong.

Ethan roared and pushed himself off the fence, one fist raised, and the other arm reached for Raine. Another punch landed on Raine's cheek, splitting the skin, and Ethan grabbed Raine by the back of the neck to deliver a follow-up strike to his mouth. Raine tasted blood and turned his face away from the next punch, leaving it to strike his ear. Cheek and mouth bleeding, ear ringing, Raine lunged forward and grabbed Ethan around the waist, if only to protect his face and try to gain a moment to catch his breath.

Ethan delivered a series of blows to the back of Raine's head, dizzying him. He needed to turn the tables and quickly. He stuck a leg between Ethan's feet and twisted their bodies, pushing Ethan off balance and sending them both to the ground again. Ethan landed on his side, and Raine rolled on top of him. Raine directed a series of punches at Ethan's head, landing several on his face and ears. He needed to end the fight. He was getting exhausted. Blood was dripping from his face, mixed with sweat and rain. Sommers was screaming something, but he couldn't make it out over the throbbing in his ears.

Then Ethan punched Raine full force in the center of his face.

Raine fell limp to the pavement. His eyes were open, but he couldn't see anything but a narrow tunnel of wet street. He tried to push himself to his feet again, but his arms didn't respond. He expected to feel Ethan's fist or foot in his face, but instead he heard the sound of glass falling to pavement and a panicked shriek from Sommers.

That last sound stirred Raine to raise his head. The tunnel vision widened enough to see Ethan holding Sommers against the building wall, one hand on her throat, the other pulled back in a trembling fist.

"This is all your fault!" he shouted in Sommers's face. "You brought him here! You think you're better than all the rest of us! You win all the awards! You play lawyer and think you can get away with anything, while the rest of us get fired because of people like you and your lawyer boyfriend. Well, not anymore! Not anymore!"

Sommers tried to argue back, but her throat was being crushed in Ethan's fat hand. "Stop," she wheezed. "Ethan, stop. Please."

Ethan was in no mind to stop. To the contrary, he was out of his right mind.

Raine knew what he had to do. He picked up one of

Sommers's dropped crystal statues and smashed it into the back of Ethan's skull. If they couldn't reason with his brain, they needed to turn it off.

Raine's fists hadn't been enough to stop a drunken and enraged Ethan Fassbinder, but ten pounds of tempered glass were. The crystal didn't shatter, like a television wine bottle prop would have. Glass was hard, and several pounds of glass delivered to the back of the head was enough to impact the brain even through the thickness of a skull. Ethan collapsed onto the pavement, unconscious. Hopefully, only unconscious.

Sommers grabbed her throat and gasped for air. "Thanks. I owe you one." Then, after a moment, "I hate owing people one."

Raine just nodded, panting. He dropped his hands to his sides and let the award drop to the pavement again. Chipped perhaps, but mostly intact.

"What the hell just happened?" Sommers croaked when she was able to speak again.

"I won a fight against a man bigger and younger than me," Raine answered.

"That's your takeaway?" Sommers screamed.

Raine shrugged. "It's one of them." He wiped his face and looked down at his blood-covered palm. "We should leave."

"Is he going to be okay?" Sommers asked.

Raine wasn't overly concerned with Ethan's condition. But he should probably make sure Ethan was still breathing. Walking away from a homicide, even a justifiable one, was a step too far. Raine got just close enough to confirm Ethan's chest was rising and falling. He was facedown but not in a puddle. He would probably be alright, eventually. It wasn't as if Raine had gotten in very many good punches.

"He's alive," Raine reported.

"We can't just leave him here," Sommers said.

Raine, to his own chagrin, agreed. He reached out to take back his jacket, wiped the blood from his face with it, then pounded on the back door to the event venue. When there was no immediate response, he pounded again, louder and longer.

After a few more moments, a young and kind-looking member of the waitstaff opened the door a crack. "Hello?"

Raine pointed down at Ethan. "This man was just at your awards gala. He's very drunk and passed out in your alleyway. You probably overserved him. You should help him if you don't want to get sued."

The young waiter's eyes widened. "Sued?"

"Yeah, lawyers suck, am I right?" Raine laughed. He could feel the blood trickling down his cheek again. He turned away from the door and waved over his shoulder. "Bye!"

He started to walk briskly away. Sommers gathered up her awards and ran after him.

"That's it?" she asked when she caught up to him. "It's over?"

"Probably not," Raine knew. "But it's over for tonight."

## 23

Monday morning arrived, and Raine showed up for court with a still swollen lip and a butterfly bandage holding the skin together under his black eye.

Chapman took one look at him and exclaimed, "What the hell happened to you?"

Raine winked at him, a painful action as it turned out. "I didn't have the kids this weekend."

That left Chapman speechless, which was always an accomplishment.

Raine's resultant smile also tugged painfully at the half-healed laceration inside his lip. It was worth it.

"Wow," Adam said as his lawyer sat down next to him. "I hope you won the fight."

"I did." Raine nodded. "Now, let's win this one."

It was a good line. The kind of line a lawyer loves to give and a client loves to hear. Raine meant it too, and not just because of lingering bravado from winning a fight over a superior, if inebriated, opponent.

The hearing was on his motion to dismiss. His motion was based on the law. And the law was clear. You had to outlive someone by one hundred twenty hours in order to inherit from that person. The Survival Rule wasn't some judicially crafted remedy from ten years ago. It was codified almost a century earlier in the Uniform Simultaneous Death Act, which in turn was based on the ancient legal principle of "death by common disaster". There were a myriad of reasons for the rule, not least of which was to reduce litigation like the one brought by Sarah Harper. If every death required a full trial to determine who died in what order and who should inherit what, the courts would be even more overwhelmed than they already were. The law was well reasoned, well established, and well tested. All Raine had to do was to convince the smartest judge in the county to follow the law.

But sometimes smart people were too smart for their own good. Or the good of those around them. Or before them.

"All rise!" the bailiff called out. "The King County Superior Court is now in session! The Honorable Veronica Fairfax presiding!"

Judge Fairfax emerged from her chambers to find the assembled lawyers and parties and court staff standing for her entrance. "Please be seated," she instructed.

A bit to Raine's surprise, Chapman complied this time. Perhaps he was still stunned by Raine's appearance. If so, Raine would have to remember that and perhaps get into a fight the night before the trial. Anything to throw off an opponent. But then again, if the hearing went as it should, there would never be a trial anyway.

"Are the parties ready in the matter of *Harper versus*

*Harper ex rel. Harper?*" the judge asked. Nothing confusing about that case title at all.

Chapman stood up to address the Court first. The plaintiff always went first. "Ms. Harper and I are ready, Your Honor."

Raine stood up next. You always stood up to speak to the judge. "The defendant is ready as well, Your Honor."

Judge Fairfax nodded. "Good. The Court is ready as well. This is a motion to dismiss under Civil Rule 12(b)(6), for failure to state a legal claim upon which relief can be granted. I have read all of the briefing and reviewed every case, statute, and secondary source cited in the briefs. I am ready to hear oral argument. This is the defendant's motion, so I will hear first from the defense. Whenever you are ready, Mr. Raine."

There was an old saying in the legal community: "If the facts are against you, pound the law. If the law is against you, pound the facts. And if they're both against you, pound the table." The facts and the law were both very much on his side, so he would pound on both. He expected Chapman would have no choice but to brutalize his table.

"Thank you," Raine began. He eschewed the formal, and in his opinion archaic, introduction of "May it please the Court." He expected Chapman to use it. All the more reason to avoid it. "This motion is based on well-established, black-letter law and indisputable facts. The law is the Survival Rule, which states that a beneficiary must survive a grantor by one hundred and twenty hours in order to inherit a bequest from the grantor. The facts are that Mark Harper, the plaintiff's late husband and the potential beneficiary of his father's will, died approximately one hundred hours after his father's death. Therefore, the Survival Rule bars the potential bequest to him. Accordingly, the property never entered into his own estate and cannot be passed via his will to his wife, the plaintiff."

That was pretty much the argument, but there was that whole thing about putting on a show to impress the client. And justify the fee.

"So let's take a moment to consider the policy considerations behind the Survival Rule," Raine considered. "I don't think it's necessary to do so, strictly speaking. The Court can and should simply accept and impose the law. But to the extent that the plaintiff is asking the Court to depart from established law, it is worth considering why it would be inadvisable to do so."

Raine then launched into an explanation of the Survival Rule. He began with its formative beginnings in English common law and followed the line all the way into modern American statutory law. The law was the law and had long been the law. It wasn't the most interesting topic to the average person, or even the average lawyer, but he thought Judge Fairfax might enjoy the lecture. And she was his audience.

"So, in summary," Raine concluded, "the history of the law in this area leads to the only allowable legal conclusion. Mark Harper did not survive William Harper by one hundred and twenty hours. Therefore, Mark Harper did not inherit the Harper Development Corporation from William Harper, Sarah Harper cannot inherit the corporation from Mark, and Adam Harper inherits the corporation as the only son who, legally speaking, survived his father. Thank you."

Raine sat down and looked to his client for some sort of favorable reaction.

"That was a lot of law words." Adam frowned.

Raine's expression dropped a bit as well. Adam wasn't wrong. "Well, it's a technical legal area. I'm sure the judge was able to follow along."

A glance up to Judge Fairfax confirmed her expression was one of complete comprehension. Raine hoped that meant it was also one of agreement. But she hadn't heard everything yet.

"Mr. Chapman." The judge invited his response. "Whenever you're ready."

Chapman stood up, buttoned his suit coat, and threw an arm wide at Raine. "We greatly appreciate Mr. Raine's legal history lecture, but this isn't a case about the past. It's a case about the present. It's a case about real people. It's a case about Sarah Harper, her husband Mark, and his father William. It's a case about what they would have wanted to happen to their family business. And it's a case that gives this Court an opportunity to make sure that what William Harper and Mark Harper wanted becomes reality. It's a case about fairness, and ultimately it's a case about justice. This Court has no higher calling."

Raine's frown deepened. That was a pretty good opening salvo. He was glad they weren't in front of a jury. A judge was less likely to be swayed by clever advocacy... he hoped.

"In this case, it can hardly be argued that William Harper did not want his company to go to his younger son, Adam Harper," Chapman continued. "In fact, at the time of his death, he was engaged in a lawsuit to prevent that very thing from happening, and upon the filing of that lawsuit, he changed his will so that the company, rather than being bequeathed jointly to his two sons, would go only to his older child, Mark. Adam's interest in the company was reduced from a full share to a conditional share. He would only inherit if Mark died first, and then only to prevent the company from going to no one and having to be liquidated.

It was never the intent of William Harper that Adam inherit under these circumstances, and to apply the law in such a way as to effectuate the outcome sought by the defendant would be the exact opposite of everything William Harper wished when he executed his last will and testament days before his tragic and untimely death."

Raine supposed that was true. But the law was still the law.

"We should also take a moment to consider what Mark Harper would have wanted to happen to the company," Chapman asserted.

Raine wasn't convinced that was actually relevant, but he wasn't about to interrupt. It wasn't professional to interrupt opposing counsel's argument. More importantly, Judge Fairfax wouldn't have liked it.

"Mark Harper," Chapman continued, "was a loving and devoted husband. He and Sarah never had children, but they had a wonderful marriage. His own will was simple and sweet. Everything went to Sarah. Everything. And that everything should have included his share in the Harper Development Corporation. Had Adam Harper not gotten impatient and greedy, prompting their father to change his will, Mark's share would have been half of the company, and then, eventually, upon his death, Sarah would have received that half share. But when Adam filed his lawsuit, and William changed his will, that half share became a whole share. And I can tell you with absolute certainty that William Harper would have preferred his company to stay in the hands of extended family who was loyal to him than go to a son who betrayed him."

"I was just trying to do what was best for the company," Adam protested to Raine in a hushed voice.

Raine nodded. "I know."

"Tell the judge that," Adam directed.

"I will," Raine agreed.

And he would. Chapman was trying to pull on the judge's heartstrings. Raine wasn't convinced Judge Fairfax really had heartstrings that a lawyer appearing before her could pull on. However, in the event he was mistaken, Raine wasn't going to allow Chapman to be the only one to do it.

But it wasn't his turn yet to speak again.

"And so the Court appears to be faced with an impossible decision," Chapman posited. "Follow the law, or follow the intent of the grantor, which the law is supposed to support above all else. The highest goal of any court is justice, and justice in this case is to give meaning and effect to what William Harper would have wanted. My worthy opponent argues that the Court is prohibited from doing so. Prohibited from doing justice. But I say, where justice is concerned, there is always a way."

Chapman was using the amorphous concept of "justice" as a substitute for that table he was supposed to be pounding on. Smart, Raine supposed, but the law was still on his side, and wasn't the result the law dictated, by definition, justice. He frowned. Not always, he knew. He'd need better for his rebuttal argument.

"There is another aspect to justice which the Court must consider," Chapman went on, "when considering the defendant's motion to dismiss this case prior to trial, and that aspect is the equitable doctrine of unjust enrichment."

*Oh boy, here we go*, Raine thought. He glanced at his

client to see if he knew what was coming. His placid expression suggested he did not.

"It is a long-standing principle of the law," Chapman declared, "longer even than the doctrines that gave rise to the Survival Rule upon which Mr. Raine relies, that a person may not benefit from his own wrong deeds. There are examples everywhere in the law, from contract law to the evidence rules. You can't break a contract and expect to receive the benefits of it. You can't arrange for a witness to be absent from trial and then complain if their hearsay statements are admitted instead. And in the context of inheritance law, you can't inherit from a grantor if you had a hand in that grantor's death."

Now it was time to interrupt opposing counsel.

"Objection!" Raine jumped to his feet. "This is nothing short of the worst kind of innuendo and character assassination. There is no evidence that my client had anything to do with his father's untimely demise. To the contrary, he had just initiated a complex and lengthy litigation against him, evincing his expectation that his father would live for some time to come, to the detriment of their family business."

"Mr. Raine?" Judge Fairfax looked down at him.

"Yes, Your Honor?" Raine answered.

"You will get your turn to reply," the judge said. "Now, sit down. This is argument. Objection overruled."

Raine sighed and sat down again, but his client patted him on the back, appreciating the effort. That was part of why he did it.

"Please continue, Mr. Chapman," the judge encouraged.

Chapman took a moment to gather his thoughts. "Mr. Raine's outburst makes me think this might be a good time to stop and note the nature of today's motion, and the standard to be applied in deciding such a motion. This is a motion to dismiss my client's lawsuit and thereby prevent it from ever being presented to a jury for determination of the merits of its claims. A court should only grant such a motion if there is no material dispute as to the law or the facts. The Court can only grant this motion to dismiss if it finds that no reasonable jury could possibly rule in favor of the plaintiff, when looking at the plaintiff's allegations in the light most favorable to the plaintiff. Otherwise, the Court should deny the motion and let the jury decide. Another bedrock principle of our justice system: let the jury decide.

"Here, Mr. Raine's objection just puts a spotlight on a very important factual disagreement in this case. My client believes and asserts that Adam Harper had something to do with the deaths of William Harper and/or Mark Harper. The law is clear that if he was responsible for his father's death, then he cannot inherit from him. Likewise, if he had something to do with his brother's death, then he should not receive the benefit of that death occurring at a moment in time that might otherwise benefit him."

Raine knew the first part about inheritance law—Adam couldn't inherit from his father if he murdered him. The second assertion was less clear. There wasn't really any law on what happens if you murder your brother just in the nick of time to claw back his inheritance for yourself. But Raine could guess how that might play out.

"Unlike the defendant, we are not asking the Court to decide the entire case right now," Chapman explained. "We are asking the Court to allow a jury to decide later. This is an important case. It deals with substantial assets, and it involves complex and novel issues of the law. We say William Harper would not have wanted his company to go to his son

Adam. We say that's especially true given the suspicious circumstances surrounding his and his son Mark's deaths. We say let the jury decide. Please, Your Honor. Deny this motion and let the jury decide. That would be justice. Thank you." Chapman sat down to the whispered accolades of his client.

Judge Fairfax swiveled her head, owl-like, to look down at the defendant's table. "Any reply, Mr. Raine?"

It was Raine's motion, which meant he got to go first, and he got to go last. It was a way to keep both sides honest—at least honest for lawyers. Chapman would at least know that Raine would have a chance to respond to anything he said. He couldn't claim just anything without fear of contradiction.

"Yes, Your Honor. Thank you." Raine stood up and straightened his suit jacket. The reply argument was meant to be shorter, limited to actual responses to the points raised by the other attorney. It was not an opportunity for another speech. That was fine with Raine. He didn't much like a legal history lecture either.

"Justice," he began. "That's an important word. An important concept. It's the reason all of us are here today. It's the reason we do the jobs we do. It is a noble calling and an elusive goal. I agree with my worthy opponent that the Court should seek justice. How could I not? But where I disagree, and where the Court should disagree, is the assertion that justice requires every case, however frivolous, to go to a jury. It is not justice to subject a defendant to the risk of an unjust verdict. It is not justice to subject a defendant to the time, expense, and indignities of litigation just because the other side doesn't like the law. Justice is the goal, yes, but the law is our tool to create justice. When the law is clear, then it is unjust to allow a case to go forward, to allow a plaintiff to drag a defendant through the court system for no greater reason than that the plaintiff had the temerity to file a quixotic lawsuit. When that happens, when a plaintiff attempts to use the court system to harass a defendant who should and will prevail under the settled law, then there are systems in place to protect the defendant and terminate the lawsuit. Then, Your Honor, justice requires one thing: dismissal."

Raine took a moment to gauge how his argument was being received. Adam nodded up encouragingly at him. Chapman was frowning down at his notepad. Sarah was glaring at him through narrowed eyes. Those were all good. The one that mattered was Judge Fairfax, and her expression was utterly blank.

"My client was in the middle of probating his father's estate, as required by his father's will," Raine continued, "when this lawsuit was filed. Now, everything is on hold until this litigation is terminated. There are costs to litigation, Your Honor. We all know that. I'm not doing this for free, and neither is Mr. Chapman. Your Honor and your staff have other cases waiting to use this courtroom. Workers and vendors and contractors are going unpaid while a half-finished skyscraper blights the downtown skyline.

"If we all had infinite resources and we could do the entire trial in an hour, then maybe it would be worth allowing the case to proceed, as Mr. Chapman implores. But time and money are very real concerns, and this court does not exist to humor every claim by every plaintiff who feels aggrieved by the way fate has unfolded. Indeed, Your Honor, the Survival Rule was adopted specifically to prevent litigation like this. So let it do its job. Stop this unfounded litigation and dismiss this lawsuit. That's the law. And that, in turn, is justice. Thank you." Raine sat down again, to hushed accolades of his own client.

Chapman obviously wanted to respond, but that wasn't how it worked. It was the judge's turn to speak. Raine hoped for the best.

"Thank you," Judge Fairfax said. "Thank you to both, counsel. I appreciate your advocacy and will take your arguments under advisement."

Raine stifled a sigh. That was right. Fairfax never issued a decision from the bench. It was a sign that she liked to be certain and wanted a moment to reflect on and reach the proper conclusion. It also meant she didn't want to argue with the lawyer who lost, a common occurrence with the vast majority of judges, who were usually ready to rule before the lawyers said the first word, let alone after they had had their say. Those judges saw sparring with losing counsel as part of the job. Fairfax saw it as unpleasant and unnecessary.

Raine stood up again. "Thank you, Your Honor."

"Sit down, Mr. Raine," the judge instructed. Not harshly, but matter-of-factly. "I'm not done yet."

Raine did as he was told. That was what he got for trying to be polite.

"It has been impressed upon me, repeatedly, by counsel for the defendant, that time is of the essence," Judge Fairfax said. "Counsel for the plaintiff seems to be in less of a hurry, although certainly that is related to the current posture of the litigation."

Raine wondered where she was going with all of that. Chapman seemed to have a puzzled look on his face too, although Raine couldn't be sure. He always thought Chapman looked dumb.

"The issue of time has been on my mind since it was raised at the last hearing," the judge continued, "and it was raised again today. I do not like to issue rulings from the bench; however, I am considering doing so if both lawyers can assure me that I will not be interrupted, contradicted, argued with, or subjected to any other connivance, entreaty, or plea."

Raine's eyes lit up. Could he really be done with the case that day? Get back to the drudgery of finishing the probating of the estate and free up a weekend night to see Sawyer again?

"I can give that assurance," he quickly rose to say.

Chapman followed suit. "I as well, Your Honor."

They both sat down again and prepared for the judge's ruling.

Judge Fairfax seemed to be bracing herself as well. She took a deep breath and began. "Counsel for the plaintiff is correct that the Survival Rule is established law. He is also correct that one of the reasons for the adoption of that rule is to reduce litigation. Dismissing this case at this time would serve that purpose."

Raine liked where the judge was heading so far.

"Counsel for the defendant asks the Court to ignore the rule because it would frustrate the will of the grantor. Whether he is correct about that, I am unsure. I doubt William Harper anticipated the events of his own and then his elder son's death. However, it doesn't matter because I am not going to ignore established law. And certainly not on the record before me now."

Raine allowed a smile. Maybe Sawyer would even be free that night.

"It is also established law that when there is a material dispute as to the facts of a case, and those facts could impact the ultimate verdict, then it would be inappropriate for the Court to terminate the litigation early."

*Uh-oh.* Raine's heart sank. He looked at Adam, who was still smiling, but only because he didn't know what the judge was about to say. Chapman was smiling too, because he did.

"I do not have sufficient facts before me today to determine whether there is any merit to the plaintiff's assertions that the defendant has unclean hands as it pertains to the deaths of his father and brother," the judge continued.

"Damn right," Adam whispered confidently, and mistakenly so.

"But that insufficiency of facts is in itself a fact for the purposes of today's hearing on the defendant's motion to dismiss," Judge Fairfax explained. "There is a factual issue about which the parties disagree. This factual issue could impact the outcome of the litigation. Therefore, I am denying the defendant's motion to dismiss."

"What?" Adam called out.

Raine grabbed at him, but he was already standing up.

"Are you kidding me?" Adam shouted. "You believe what that slimeball attorney said about me killing my dad? My brother?"

Fairfax recoiled from the outburst. "This—this is why I don't—" she stammered. Then she shook her head and stood up. "Court is adjourned," she declared and escaped into her chambers.

The bailiff gave out an, "All rise!" but it was unnecessary.

Adam and Raine were already on their feet, and the judge was already gone.

Raine grabbed Adam by the shoulders. "Stop! Right now!"

"But she ruled against us!" Adam shook a fist at the bench where the judge had been. His eyes were wide, and his chest was heaving. Not a good look for someone who said he didn't have anything to do with his family members' demises.

"Yes, she did," Raine acknowledged. "And you need to calm down, or she will rule against us for the entire rest of the case."

Adam's eyebrows knitted together. That seemed to make sense to him. He relaxed slightly. "But she's wrong. I didn't do any of what they're saying."

"I know," Raine assured him.

But Adam scowled. "You think I did it too. You accused me of it too."

"I asked you," Raine clarified. "Specifically because of what the other side was going to say and what the judge might think about it."

Adam shook his head. "No. No, you think I did it too."

"I don't think anything," Raine answered. "I'm a lawyer. I believe my client until there's evidence I shouldn't, and even after that sometimes. But now is not the time for this. We have trial coming up and coming up fast. Do you want to win the trial?"

Adam's scowl softened slightly. "Yes."

"Of course you do," Raine replied. "So stop yelling at judges and get the hell out of the courthouse before the bailiff calls a marshal to arrest you for threatening a judge."

"I didn't threaten her," Adam protested.

"I can assure you that she felt threatened," Raine replied. "Now, leave. I will schedule a meeting with you to discuss trial strategy, but now is not the time."

Adam just stood there.

"Leave," Raine repeated.

Adam nodded then and turned to make his way out of the courtroom.

Raine turned to see what Chapman was doing, but to his surprise he was alone in the courtroom. The court staff had followed immediately after the judge, and Chapman and Sarah must have slipped out while Raine was calming Adam down.

Raine allowed himself a lengthy sigh, then started packing up his things. That probably could not have gone worse. Fairfax was probably going to have an armed marshal in the courtroom for every subsequent hearing, and there was no way they were going to win any of the close calls. That was bad news because a lot of times, whoever won the close calls ended up winning the whole case. The only good news was that Adam's outburst had made everyone forget about Chapman's request for an injunction to prevent Adam from taking any actions with the company. Not that that really mattered: he wasn't taking any actions anyway.

Raine glanced around the courtroom one more time. He imagined there must be a job that didn't involve taking on other people's stress for a living. But he supposed it probably wasn't as interesting. And he'd only lost one motion, after all.

"There's plenty more to lose before the case is over," he joked to himself as he headed to the exit.

The joke didn't help his mood much, however. The worst part of losing was that he lost to Chapman. It would just confirm in Chapman's mind that he was the better attorney. Back in law school, he'd always acted like he was better than Raine. If landing at the fancy firm, able to buy fancy suits and fancy cars, hadn't confirmed Chapman's sense of superiority already, winning that motion was sure to do it for him. Maybe he and Natalie could talk about it over dinner that weekend.

He opened the door to the hallway a crack, but then stopped when he heard Chapman talking to Sarah.

"We got lucky today," he said, "but make no mistake, that guy is one hell of an attorney. He's going to learn from this, and he's going to be prepared when it's time for trial. The one thing standing between you and Harper Development is Daniel Raine."

## 24

Despite the loss, Raine was in the mood to celebrate. Chapman's overheard assessment of him gave him new life. He called Sawyer, but she wasn't available on a Monday night with no notice. The coming weekend was out too because Raine had his boys, and he wasn't ready to start introducing them to a series of rotating girlfriends. He didn't want to be that divorced dad.

So it wasn't until the following weekend that they made plans for a wine-tasting date on the other side of Lake Washington, in Woodinville, a northeastern suburb that had managed not only to cultivate grapes in Seattle's northern climate, but turn the wineries into a romantic attraction for curious tourists and local couples. Couples who liked wine, anyway. Or Central California transplants who couldn't believe wine grown in the shadow of the Space Needle could be any good and wanted to see for themselves.

They had driven separately due to their incongruous work schedules. Raine had been in his Seattle office the entire afternoon. Sawyer had had hearings in Kent, a city twenty miles south of Seattle where the county had put a second courthouse to deal with the burgeoning population and resultant increase in everything, including crime. It didn't make sense for either of them to pick up the other.

Raine arrived in the suit he wore that day, but Sawyer had obviously stopped somewhere to change. He found her waiting at an outside table, dressed completely, almost extremely, femininely. She wore a flower-print sundress, a sun hat with a wide lavender ribbon, and white sandals.

"I like your outfit," he said as he walked up.

Sawyer looked down at her ensemble. "Too much?"

"More like too little," Raine answered. "It isn't July in Napa. Aren't you cold?"

"This is my winery outfit," Sawyer answered. "One of them anyway. It's not my fault it's too cold up here."

"We could go inside," Raine suggested.

"You could shut up and sit down," Sawyer counteroffered. "I'm fine. I don't need you to police my outfit. I look dazzling. Enjoy the view or move along."

Raine laughed at her directness. He sat down. "I'm not moving along."

Sawyer leaned forward and smiled at him. "Good."

Raine had never been to that particular winery/restaurant. In fact, he couldn't recall ever going to any of them except for a wedding he couldn't get out of for some reason, and that had been over a decade earlier. The wine was good, even Sawyer begrudgingly admitted that, and the food was excellent. The only real drawback, one that became frustratingly clear as the sun began to set and dinner drew to a close, was how far away it was from Seattle, and specifically either his condo or Sawyer's apartment.

"You wanna get out of here?" he asked with a suggestive grin as he put his credit card back in his wallet.

"You mean back to your place for a nightcap?" Sawyer pretended to be breathless as she asked the question. "After a twenty-minute drive?"

"Maybe thirty," Raine replied seductively. He nodded to the sky. "It's about to rain."

Sawyer broke character and shook her head. "Damn. We should get out of here, then. Text me your address. Is there any parking?"

Raine shrugged as he stood up from the table. "Sometimes. You might need to circle the block a couple of times."

"Foreplay," Sawyer quipped. "Perfect."

"We could drive together," Raine proffered.

"And have to come back and get one of our cars from the other side of the county? No, thanks." Sawyer shot down the idea. "I'll just meet you at your place. It'll be worth it, I promise."

Raine had no doubt about that. Despite weeks of dating, they had managed somehow to fail to consummate their relationship. He considered suggesting a room at the nearest Woodinville hotel, but he didn't want to seem desperate. He was, but desperation was the opposite of sexy.

"I'm going to hold you to that promise," Raine told her.

"That's not the only thing you're going to be holding tonight," she teased.

Raine was really looking forward to getting home. The rain was starting to fall, those fat droplets that warned the coming storm would be heavy. Sawyer had parked right next to the restaurant; the closest spot Raine could find was across the street and halfway up the block. He walked her to her car, texted her the address, then hurried to his own car as she pulled out of the parking lot. He still wished they had driven together—they could have messed around a little on the drive—but the rain was settling in fast, so it probably wouldn't have been safe anyway. He just needed to put the wipers on high and drive rapidly but safely to his condo, where Sawyer would be waiting for them to finally spend a night together.

The last leg of Raine's trip home was the Evergreen Point Floating Bridge. The bridge deck rested directly on top of Lake Washington, the seventeen-mile-long, three-mile-wide, and two-hundred-foot-deep lake that separated Seattle from the suburbs on the "Eastside". By the time Raine reached the bridge, the rain was coming down in sheets. He could barely see the distant red lights of the cars already out on the bridge. Traffic was light, probably because people were waiting out the storm. He squinted through the blur of his windshield wipers, trying to make out the lane dividers on the narrow four-lane, no-shoulder bridge. He suddenly became very aware of how low the guardrail was between his speeding car and the churning black depths of the lake.

Raine's focus on his precarious surroundings was diverted by a new concern: a pair of headlights approaching rapidly in his rearview mirror. They were on bright, as well. He squinted against the glare and flipped the mirror to dim the glow, but the headlights continued to barrel down on him. He checked his own speed. He was going 40 mph, which was probably too fast for the road and weather conditions. The approaching car must have been going 60 mph or more. He tapped twice on the brake to flash his brake lights at the approaching car.

The other westbound lane was empty; the car could

easily go around him on the left. But the approaching car didn't slow at all.

Raine was getting concerned when something even worse happened. The vehicle got within just a few car lengths of him, then turned its lights off completely. Raine braced for a rear impact collision, but then caught a glimpse of the car swinging around him at the last second. He relaxed slightly. He shouldn't have.

The car was a sleek black sedan. Raine couldn't make out the exact make or model, but it was nicer than anything he'd ever owned. It sped just past him, then swerved in front of him and slammed on its brakes.

Raine stomped on his own brake to avoid crashing into the car. The rear of his vehicle fishtailed on the wet pavement. He spun the wheel to one side, then the other and barely regained control of his car.

The darkened vehicle in front of him sped ahead, but then changed into the inside lane and braked again. Raine pulled up alongside it before he could decide to slow down himself, and the car swerved at him, pushing him toward that increasingly inadequate-looking guardrail. He swerved to his right to avoid being struck, but stopped short of hitting the guardrail. The other car swerved at him once more, and again Raine swerved away, barely avoiding a collision. He looked ahead, hoping they might be over land soon, but they were still only halfway across the bridge.

The car pulled ahead and jerked almost completely into Raine's lane, clipping his front end and sending his car spinning on the drenched bridge deck.

He smashed into the guardrail and felt the car flip into the air. Time slowed. He fully expected to land in the water. His panicked brain tried to remember whether you were supposed to roll down the windows when your car started to sink into a lake. He would only have seconds to remember. He hoped his seatbelt would unlatch.

It was really dark.

He didn't want to die.

## 25

The car landed on its roof and skidded sideways down the guardrail, sending sparks flying into the night. It came to a rest several hundred feet short of the end of the bridge, but still on the deck.

Raine hung upside down by his seatbelt. His heart was racing, and his mouth was completely dry. His arms were shaking from the adrenaline. After a few moments, he tried the seatbelt release button. It didn't work. Probably from the strain of his weight. He tried not to imagine what would have happened if he'd been strapped into his seat as the car sank in two hundred feet of water. He imagined it anyway.

After a moment, he used one arm to push off the roof of the car and tried the seatbelt release again. It worked, and he fell awkwardly onto his neck. He twisted himself into a less awkward pile and sat up slightly. Other cars started to stop, and he heard a voice calling out to ask if he was okay.

His phone was resting next to him on the upside-down roof. It lit up. He looked at the screen. There was a text from Sawyer.

I'm here. Where are you?

He picked up the phone and tapped a reply with shaking fingers.

You're not going to believe this...

---

"YOU NEED to go to the police."

Sommers was more agitated than Raine had ever seen her before. He appreciated that. But he didn't necessarily agree with her.

Raine hadn't told her about the accident until the following Monday. He didn't want to bother her on the weekend. There wasn't anything she could have done anyway. He assured her that it would definitely not affect his ability to proceed to trial as scheduled on the Harper case. She hung up on him and drove directly to his office.

"The police came to the scene," he explained. "I told them everything I could, which wasn't much. The car had its lights off. I couldn't see the license plate, and all I could tell them about the car was that it was black."

The night had not gone as planned. Sawyer tried to come back to see him, but the road was closed off for the investigation, and eventually Raine told her to go home, and they would try again another night. He wasn't in any shape for anything after the crash anyway. He didn't break any bones, but there were extensive "soft tissue injuries", as the personal injury lawyers called it. His neck and back hurt especially. And he suffered some superficial cuts to his hands and face from the shattering of the windows. The cops took forever to complete their investigation. He spent three hours on a cold and rainy bridge with nothing but a thin wool blanket to keep warm. One of the cops gave him a ride home, and when he got upstairs, the only thing he wanted to do was sleep. He'd wash the blood out of the sheets later.

"Not those cops," Sommers answered. "That detective looking into Bill and Mark Harper's deaths. This has to be related."

Raine thought it was probably connected too, although he had certainly angered a lot of people over his career. Another intrinsic aspect of being a lawyer.

"It could have been a lot of people," he argued.

"Like Adam," Sommers accused.

"Or Ethan," Raine returned. "Or any number of people I've pissed off over the years."

Sommers offered a begrudging nod.

"I don't know." Raine rubbed the back of his still stiff neck. "What am I going to say? Here's an attack to add to what might or might not be two other attacks, which might or might not have been committed by my client, so I can't really talk about it anyway?"

"Yes, that." Sommers pointed at him. "Exactly that."

Raine sighed and shook his head.

"Come on." Sommers gestured for him to stand up and follow her. "I'll drive."

---

"MR. RAINE?" A uniformed officer opened a secure door to the lobby of the Seattle Police Department's downtown precinct. "Detective Kavendish will see you now."

Raine was a bit surprised. He'd expected to be dismissed with little to no ceremony. Detectives came to talk to you, not the other way around. He had explained the reason for his visit to a different officer sitting behind bulletproof glass at a sort of reception desk, if the receptionists all wore body armor and carried handguns and Tasers. The armed receptionist told him to have a seat while he tried to contact the detective. Raine and Sommers did just that, and it was less than five minutes before Raine was being bid into the interior of the precinct.

Sommers patted him on the back as he stood up. He winced, still sore from the accident.

"Good luck," she said.

He just turned and offered a pained smile and thumbs-up.

The police officer led him through the cubicle-lined hallways, to a secure elevator that required a flash of a police ID badge, then down another corridor of cubicles, and finally to a small, interior office with the nameplate "Michael Kavendish" on the door. The officer departed, and Raine stepped uneasily inside, awaiting a greeting from the detective, whose face was lowered, examining a file on his desk.

He gestured toward his one guest chair without looking up. "Have a seat, Mr. Raine. I'm just reviewing the file."

"So you remember me?" Raine asked as he lowered himself gingerly into the metal and vinyl chair.

"Hard to forget a lawyer present at not one but two deaths." Kavendish finally looked up. "Are you here to tell me something you didn't tell me before?"

"Well, sort of," Raine answered, "but only because it hadn't happened yet."

Kavendish narrowed his eyes at him. "Your face is cut up.

Did you fall off a building too? Although, a shorter one, I would gather."

Raine didn't really appreciate the attempt at humor. "No. Someone tried to run me off the road. Into Lake Washington, to be specific. I think it might be related."

Kavendish leaned back and thought for a moment. "Which bridge?"

"Five-Twenty." Raine answered with the freeway number.

"Eastbound or westbound?"

"Westbound."

"Were you still out over the water?"

"Yes," Raine confirmed. "That's why I said they tried to run me into the lake."

Kavendish nodded. "Sorry, not my jurisdiction. Maybe if you'd made it to Montlake Avenue," referencing the first exit on the Seattle side of the bridge.

"Well, that was my intent," Raine replied. "But I'm not asking you to investigate it. The State Patrol did a wonderful job of closing off the road for several hours while they confirmed that my car was totaled."

"Then what do you want me to do exactly?" the detective asked.

Raine wasn't entirely sure either. Sommers should have come back with him. "I wanted you to know because I think it's probably related to the Harper case. Maybe we could exchange information or something."

"You want me to exchange information with a suspect?" Kavendish laughed.

Raine took a beat. "Suspect? I'm a suspect?"

Kavendish shrugged. "You were present at the time and location of both deaths."

"That's a coincidence," Raine defended. "And hardly a basis to make someone a suspect. It's a busy intersection. There were probably other people who were in the vicinity both times."

"Like your girlfriend, Ms. Mount?" Kavendish suggested.

Raine raised a finger at the detective. "First of all, she's not my girlfriend." *Despite repeated efforts*, he thought to himself. "Second, I don't think we need to bring her into it."

"Okay, fine," Kavendish agreed. "What about your client? Adam Harper. Would you like to share some information about him? He seems like a pretty likely suspect too."

"Well, obviously I can't share information about a client with law enforcement," Raine scoffed.

"Exactly," Kavendish replied.

"Wait." Raine realized something. "Why are you talking about suspects? Are you investigating the deaths as something other than accidents?"

"Are you going to tell me what your client said about them?" Kavendish asked.

Raine thought he probably could do so without doing any damage to his client. It wasn't as if Adam had confessed to murdering his father and brother, even if he hadn't explicitly denied it either. But regardless of what his client had told him, he couldn't divulge it to any third party, and especially not a cop.

"Of course not," Raine answered. "You know that."

"I do know that," the detective answered. "Just like I know your idea of exchanging information is exclusively one way. If you want to tell me something useful, I'm more than happy to listen. Hell, I'll even record it. But I'm not in the practice of sharing information with defense attorneys. Not without getting something in return."

"I'm not a defense attorney," Raine corrected him with a raised hand. "I have a general practice that sometimes includes criminal defense."

Kavendish just raised an eyebrow at him.

"I represent Mr. Harper in his current civil litigation," Raine expounded, "not any pending criminal cases. In part because there aren't any criminal cases."

"Not yet," Kavendish pointed out.

"What's that supposed to mean?" Raine asked, beginning to grow a little perturbed.

"Your guy is getting sued by his brother's widow, right?" Kavendish asked.

Raine supposed he shouldn't be surprised that a detective could figure out what was going on in a public court case. "Right."

"Is he going to testify?" Kavendish asked.

Raine hadn't completely decided yet, the trial was still a few weeks off, but it was likely. "Probably," he answered.

"Good." Kavendish clapped his hands together. "Maybe I'll come and watch. After that, you might get to represent him in a criminal case after all."

---

"How'd it go?" Sommers asked when Raine returned to the lobby.

"Not well," he answered.

Sommers was silent for a moment as they both walked toward the exit. "Now what?"

"Now"—Raine opened the door to the street—"I get back to work. I have a trial to prepare for."

## 26

There was a lot to do to prepare for a typical trial. Records requests, depositions, subpoenas. But a will contest wasn't a typical trial. No one was charged with a crime, and no one was trying to get money directly from another person for injuring them. They were really fighting over what a third person did, or didn't do, or meant, or didn't mean. The enemy wasn't a robber or a cop, a negligent driver or a quack doctor. It was a document and an archaic law. And Zac Chapman.

Raine wanted to ask his ex-wife if she had started seeing him. He wanted to know. But he also didn't want to know.

There were a lot of reasons he didn't want to know— well, one main one, but there was a secondary reason as well. If she confirmed it, then he would have to deal with whatever feelings that might or might not unleash. But if she denied it, then Raine would lose one of the reasons he really wanted to crush Chapman at the trial. He didn't want to give up any edge he might have. He could wait until the trial was over, and hopefully, if it were true, he could take solace that she was dating, in court anyway, a loser.

To help make that a reality, Raine spent the next weeks focusing almost exclusively on the Harper case, with the exception of covering mandatory hearings on cases for his few other clients. And those mostly consisted of telling everyone involved that he was about to start a trial and would be essentially unavailable once it started. That was the accepted norm among trial attorneys. Trial trumped everything.

Eventually the Friday before trial arrived, and the parties assembled once again before Judge Fairfax for the trial confirmation hearing. Given how the last hearing had ended, Raine grabbed Adam by the lapel and told him what to do when the judge came out.

"Two words. Shut the fuck up."

Before Adam could bluster a response, the bailiff stood up and called everyone to their feet. Court was in session, and Judge Fairfax was presiding.

"Please be seated," she directed in the same soft voice she always used.

Raine was watching for any sign that Adam's previous outburst would prejudice them. So far, so good, but it was a small sample size. He sat down and directed his client to do the same. Chapman was smart enough not to do anything to transfer the judge's ire from his opponent back to himself, so he and Sarah sat down quietly as well. There was definitely a feeling in the courtroom like when a parent is angry but eerily calm, and the kids are waiting to see what happens next.

"Are the parties ready on the matter of *Harper versus*

*Harper ex rel. Harper?*" Judge Fairfax asked. Always the first question. Another indicator of normality.

Raine and Chapman each stood, announced they were ready, and sat down again.

Fairfax nodded but stopped short of adding a "good" or other commentary.

"Trial is scheduled to begin on Monday," she announced, although everyone assembled knew that already. "Mr. Chapman, you represent the plaintiff, so I will ask you first. Is the plaintiff prepared to proceed to trial on Monday?"

Chapman stood up. "Yes, Your Honor."

Fairfax offered another nod, then turned to the other side. "Mr. Raine, is the defendant prepared to proceed to trial on Monday?"

Raine stood as well. "Yes, Your Honor."

"Good," the judge said. She turned to the plaintiff's table. "Mr. Chapman, are there any matters which the plaintiff feels need to be resolved before we convene on Monday morning?"

"No, Your Honor," Chapman answered.

"Mr. Raine, same question." Fairfax turned back to him. "Are there any matters which the defendant feels need to be resolved before we convene on Monday morning?"

"No, Your Honor." Raine echoed Chapman's response.

Judge Fairfax nodded again. She looked pained. Upset, but not willing to show it. Raine thought he might have preferred a scolding after all. Something to clear the air and signal that the judge had moved on. Instead, it appeared that she had not.

"Then we will reconvene Monday morning at nine o'clock sharp," the judge declared. She banged her gavel quietly atop the bench. "Court is adjourned."

Everyone stood up for the judge's exit, but after a step, she stopped and looked back down at them. "Mr. Raine?"

"Yes, Your Honor," he replied instantly.

"If your client says a single word out of turn, I will put both him and you in jail for thirty days for contempt of court," the judge said. "Is that understood?"

Raine nodded. "Perfectly, Your Honor."

Raine dropped his shoulders as the judge finally departed.

*Nothing like having a little skin in the game*, he thought.

———

THE NIGHT before trial was a special time for a trial attorney. "Sacred" was probably too strong a word, but it was a space to be protected, respected, honored even. Raine spent the afternoon double-checking every preparation so he could spend the evening in quiet reflection before going to bed early enough to get a good night's rest. Not sleep. He wouldn't be sleeping, not for any extended period anyway. But rest. So he could wake up on time, leave on time, and get to the courthouse on time.

No distractions. No boys. No Sawyer. Certainly no Natalie. No Sommers. No Ethan. Just a single glass of single malt and the quiet embrace of his own thoughts.

Except those thoughts repeatedly drifted unbidden to his boys, to Sawyer, even to Natalie.

He looked out his balcony window at his mostly obstructed view of downtown Seattle and sipped at his whiskey. Trial had a way of consuming one's thoughts.

He was looking forward to tomorrow.

## 27

Raine walked into Judge Fairfax's courtroom fifteen minutes before 9:00 to see five people he expected to see and one he was surprised, excited, and anxious—in that order—to see.

"Sawyer?" He walked up to where she was seated in the front row immediately behind the defendant's table. "What are you doing here?"

"Fangirling, I think," she answered. She wore a red blazer over a white silk shell, with striped pants and wingtips. "I didn't hear from you this weekend. Now I know why. I looked up your case schedules on the court website and saw that your trial starts today. I'm here for good luck."

Raine had to smile. He didn't know if she would really bring good luck, but he knew he liked seeing her. And he appreciated that she had been thinking about him.

"Are you going to stay for the whole trial?" he asked.

"Oh, hell no." She laughed. "I have a job too, remember? In fact, I have a hearing in ten minutes. I just wanted to wish you luck."

"Cool. Thanks."

Sawyer leaned in and glanced over at Chapman. "Is that the guy who's seeing your ex?" she whispered.

Raine realized he really needed to stop oversharing when he'd had a couple of drinks. "Yeah. I guess so. Maybe." Chapman was looking back at them, but in a way that showed he was trying not to look like he was looking at them.

"Good," Sawyer whispered. Then she leaned in and kissed Raine fully on the mouth for a few seconds. "Knock 'em dead, baby."

A smile exploded on Raine's face as he watched Sawyer retreat from the courtroom. After a moment, he regained his bearings. Courtroom. Trial. Now. He shook his head slightly and walked to the plaintiff's counsel table, where Adam sat and stared at him, open mouthed.

"Uh, Raine..." Chapman called out weakly from his spot at the table next to them. He clearly had rehearsed some trash-talk line, but was having trouble delivering it after Sawyer's public display of affection. "Another lonely weekend?"

That obviously didn't land. But Raine had anticipated something along those lines and had a response ready.

"Not really. The boys were with me. Or didn't you know that?"

He was calling Chapman's bluff and planting doubt. He figured it was pretty unlikely that Chapman had really memorized the residential schedule Raine and Natalie followed. So if he was trying to date Natalie, and she didn't call him on a weekend the boys were supposedly with Raine, then maybe she wasn't that into him after all. It wasn't about whether it was true. It was about making him think it might be true. Nagging doubt would live as a distraction a lot longer than an unwelcome fact.

Chapman didn't reply, so Raine happily turned away to check in with his client before the judge came out.

"You have some lipstick on your mouth." Adam pointed at his lawyer's face.

Raine smiled again at the memory of how he got that lipstick. He grabbed a tissue from the box on the table and wiped his mouth clean. He took a moment to stare at the fire engine red stain hue. It matched her jacket perfectly.

"Are you going to be able to focus?" Adam asked him.

A fair question, Raine supposed.

"Absolutely," he assured. Then the more important inquiry. "Are you going to be able to keep your mouth shut? I don't want to spend thirty days in jail."

Adam nodded and mimed pulling a zipper across his lips.

"Good." Raine breathed a sigh of relief. "I'm going to have enough to focus on. I don't need to worry about you being held in contempt on top of everything else."

"All rise!" bellowed the bailiff, and court was in session once again.

Judge Fairfax took the bench and got right to business. She asked if the parties were ready; they were. She moved right into scheduling, dictating the hours the trial would be in session rather than seeking input from the attorneys about their schedules. They quickly moved on to motions *in limine*, the small evidentiary rulings that didn't require testimony to decide. Witnesses were excluded from listening to each other testify; neither side could introduce self-serving hearsay; things like that.

Then she was ready to start picking a jury. Raine noticed

that she had not in fact requested an armed marshal be present in her courtroom while Adam was in it. Instead, it seemed, she had decided to simply move the trial along at breakneck speed to minimize the amount of time she was exposed to him.

It still took two days to select the jury, but at the start of the third day, everyone assembled in Judge Fairfax's courtroom, and she announced, "Ladies and gentlemen of the jury, please give your attention to Mr. Chapman, who will deliver the opening statement on behalf of the plaintiff."

The plaintiff always went first. In criminal cases, that meant the prosecution. In civil cases, it meant the plaintiff's attorney. The reason was the same. The plaintiff, whether it be the government trying to put someone in prison or a widow trying to claw her almost-inheritance back from her dead husband's brother, was the one who was asserting something. The defendant stole a computer. The other driver caused my whiplash. I should inherit a multimillion-dollar company because I don't like the law and my brother-in-law is shady. The law, criminal and civil, rested on the fundamental tenet that "who asserts must prove". And the person with the burden of proof had to lay out their case first before the defendant even had to respond. If they failed to do that, a defendant didn't need to say anything at all.

Of course, Raine was going to give an opening statement no matter how inadequate Chapman's opening statement might turn out to be. But Raine knew it wouldn't be inadequate. Chapman might have been a terrible person, but he wasn't a terrible lawyer.

"Thank you, Your Honor," Chapman said as he stood up. Then that overly formal, ingratiating, "May it please the Court, counsel, members of the jury."

He buttoned his suit coat and stepped out from behind the plaintiff's counsel table. He strode confidently into the "well", that empty area of the courtroom surrounded by the jury box, judge's bench, and counsel tables, and took up a position directly in front of the jurors, just the right distance away. Close enough to be confident, not so close as to be confrontational. A lot of being a trial lawyer was stage directions.

"Chosen family," he began. "It's a term that has gained popularity recently, especially among individuals and communities who might not be accepted by their biological families. It sounds like a contradiction. Chosen family. You're born into a family. You don't choose it. But almost all of us choose at least some portion of our family, regardless of our backgrounds or individual traits. When we fall in love and get married, we are choosing someone to become part of our family. When we fall out of love and get divorced, we are again choosing who will be in our family. Adoption and surrogacy are other examples. Happy examples.

"But there are also sad examples. Painful examples. Examples when family members have a falling-out, when they stop speaking to each other, when they cut off all ties. Like when William Harper, owner and founder of Harper Development Corporation, was forced to cut ties with his younger son"—Chapman gestured to the defendant's table —"Adam Harper."

Raine was listening to every word, jotting down the most important of them on his notepad. He had given Adam a notepad too, but mostly so he would have a way to communicate with Raine without grabbing him and whisper-shouting in his ear. But Raine wasn't watching Chapman too closely. In case any of the jurors glanced his way—and most of them would at some point—he needed to look engaged, but not worried. A lot of being a trial lawyer was body language.

"Let me back up." Chapman raised his hands conversationally and took a single step to one side. "In order to understand why William Harper would cut off his son Adam, you need to know a little bit more about the Harper family and the Harper family business. William Harper would have turned seventy-two next summer. I'll talk more in a few minutes about why he didn't make that milestone, but for now what's important is that he started working construction when he was only fifteen years old, back when you could still work that young. He was a big kid and could handle a welder like someone twice his age. He fell in love with construction, everything about it. He vowed someday he'd own his own construction company, and shortly after he turned twenty, he founded Harper Construction. He was its sole owner and sole employee, but he worked hard, and he hustled. He expanded the company into a giant corporation and eventually renamed it Harper Development. They didn't just build anymore, they did everything from the first inspiration for a new development to laying the last stone in the plaza out front. And along the way he made sure of one thing, that business he built was never going to get into the hands of greedy financiers or risky speculators or some board of directors who had never put on a hard hat. It was a family business, and it was going to stay a family business."

Chapman did not look over at Adam at that point, but several of the jurors did. They were naturally curious about the case they had been chosen to sit on, and this was the first time they were hearing any of the facts. They knew Adam was family, and they knew his dad had disowned him. They wondered why and what kind of person that made him. Hopefully, he looked average and unremarkable in his dark suit and muted tie. He wasn't some hardened criminal Raine had to dress up in a sweater vest and long sleeves to cover his prison tattoos. The jurors looked back to Chapman, and he continued.

"The business was going to stay in the Harper family, expanded first by one of those choices I mentioned earlier. William met the woman he was going to marry, Donna, shortly after he founded his company. After a brief courtship, they got married, and Donna became the first employee of Harper Construction, doing all of the office work and bookkeeping. As the business grew, Donna supervised other employees to do those tasks. They had two boys together and looked forward to the time when they could retire and leave the business they had built in the hands of their children."

He frowned. "But sometimes we don't get to choose who stays in our family. Sometimes, the choice is made for us, and it's a choice we'd never make ourselves. Donna was diagnosed with cancer when she was only fifty-two years old and passed away soon thereafter. William never remarried, but he remembered their plan to leave their business to their boys. That remained his plan until a few short months ago when, after everything he had done for those boys, everything he had built for them, everything he had entrusted them with, one of them betrayed that trust. Adam. Adam Harper."

Everyone looked at Adam that time, even Chapman. Raine went ahead and looked at his client too. It would have been unnatural not to. He offered his poor client a pat on the back and a pained, understanding frown. A lot of being a trial attorney was facial expressions.

"Adam Harper betrayed his father. Adam Harper chose an action that he knew would sever ties with his father. Adam Harper chose his family, and William Harper was no longer part of it."

*Very dramatic*, Raine had to allow.

The jurors were all leaning forward, wondering what Adam had done.

"Adam decided he didn't want to wait to inherit the business from his father," Chapman explained. "He decided he didn't want to share the business with his brother, Mark. So he decided to accuse his father of being senile and sued him to take control of the company, his company. He knew his father wasn't senile, but he filed the lawsuit anyway. He chose his family. And in response, William Harper chose too.

"Immediately after being served with Adam's lawsuit trying to steal his company away from him, William Harper changed his will. Instead of the family business going equally to Adam and Mark, it would all go to Mark. Now, neither Adam nor Mark had any children, so William did put in a backup provision that if Mark died before him, then Adam would get the family business after all. At that point, there would be no other family left anyway, and Adam's betrayal would be moot. But it's vital to recognize and understand that Adam Harper made a choice to sever himself from his father, and his father made a choice to accept that severance."

Raine finally took a moment to look over at the jury. Chapman had tried to glide past the one weakness to his case. Raine wondered if any of the jurors had caught it. He couldn't quite tell, but that was okay. He would be pointing it out shortly.

"The lawsuit Adam filed against his father," Chapman went on, "never reached a resolution. William Harper died falling from an upper floor of the half-finished Harper Tower, his latest construction project and the planned crown jewel of his illustrious career. That tragic death ended the need for the lawsuit. Adam couldn't steal the company away from his father anymore because his father didn't own it. According to the terms of his will, the entire company passed to Adam's brother, Mark, and Adam could hardly accuse him of being senile. That seems like the end of the story. That should be the end of the story. The only way Adam would have received any portion of the company was if Mark had died before his father. But Mark did not die before his father. That is an absolutely uncontroverted and incontrovertible fact. And yet here we are, in a courtroom, arguing over who should own that company when the intent and the letter of William Harper's will was clear as day."

Chapman threw his hands up. "Why? Why would there even be an issue? Well, the reason there's an issue is the same reason my client is Sarah Harper, Mark's wife, and not Mark himself. Mark died in a remarkably similar way to his father just four days later. He fell off the same unfinished office tower. Four. Days. Later. So that should be easy, right? His will left everything to his wife, Sarah. Obviously then, the company goes from William Harper to Mark Harper to Sarah Harper. And yet, as we sit here right now, Adam Harper claims he owns the company. Why? Because of an ancient and archaic legal technicality that requires a person to survive for five days after the death of someone who leaves them something in their will. If Mark had lived one more day, Sarah would be the undisputed owner of Harper Development. But because of a law crafted from a time when people died all the time of unknown causes and the exact order of death could be difficult to determine, Adam thinks he should own the company. That legal technicality is really a legal fiction. A lie. It says that if someone doesn't survive by five days, then they are considered to have died before the person who wrote the will. Before. Even though everyone knows that's not true. And if Mark had actually died before his father, then under the terms of the will, Adam inherits everything."

Chapman looked down and shook his head. "Now, I ask you, ladies and gentlemen"—he looked up again at his audience—"is that fair? Is that justice? No. Of course it's not. Adam chose his family, William Harper chose his family. And we are asking you to honor those choices, even if Adam Harper doesn't want to anymore." He turned and took a step back toward his seat.

Raine wondered whether they had decided to abandon part two of their strategy. But of course he should have known better.

Chapman stopped and turned back to the jurors. "Oh, and there's one more thing," he said as if every word and action hadn't been painstakingly designed and rehearsed. "Remember how I said a man who spent his entire life in construction fell off his own building? Remember how I said his son, also raised his entire life in the construction business, fell off the same building, and one day before the deadline he needed to survive by in order to inherit that business? That seems remarkable, doesn't it? Hard to believe. One might even say suspicious. Well, you're going to hear from a witness who is going to give their opinion about those deaths. And if you decide that Adam Harper was in any way responsible for the death of either his father or his brother, well then, that will be another reason for you to do the right thing, the just thing, and award ownership of Harper Development to Sarah Harper. Just like William Harper and Mark Harper would have wanted. Thank you."

Raine felt the urge to clap, albeit sarcastically, but he knew the jurors wouldn't appreciate it. Judge Fairfax even less so. He couldn't do his opening from a jail cell.

Judge Fairfax looked down at the jurors and instructed, "Now, ladies and gentlemen of the jury, please give your attention to Mr. Raine, who will deliver the opening statement on behalf of the defendant."

Raine stood up with a "Thank you" to the judge, but nothing more. He took up essentially the same spot in front of the jury box. It was the right place to stand. He wasn't going to avoid it just because Chapman had used it first.

"Everything Mr. Chapman just said," Raine began, "is true." A spin on an old classic. One to catch the jurors off guard and in turn be interested in what he was going to say next. "Well, almost all of it. The basic facts are all correct. William Harper founded Harper Development. He had two sons, Mark and my client, Adam. Adam filed a lawsuit earlier this year to take over decision-making authority for the company because he believed his father was no longer mentally fit to do so. His father changed his will to what Mr. Chapman described and then died shortly thereafter, again in the manner Mr. Chapman described. Adam's brother, Mark, died a few days later in a similar fashion. And based on all of that, the law dictates that Harper Development Corporation now belongs to Adam Harper."

Raine took a moment, offered a light shrug, then got to

the point. "What Mr. Chapman didn't tell you is that this outcome is in fact exactly what William Harper wanted. What Mr. Chapman didn't tell you is that this outcome is exactly what the law requires. What Mr. Chapman didn't tell you is that this outcome is presumed correct, and he and his client bear the high burden of proving otherwise. A burden they will not be able to meet."

It was important to point out the burden of proof to a jury, especially when the other side had it. But there was a risk of looking guilty if that was all you did. It was all well and good to yell, "Prove it!" to the other side, but if you didn't offer your own reasons for prevailing—what they called a "counternarrative" in criminal defense circles—then the jury would know you were guilty and just hoping the other side wouldn't be able to prove it after all.

"And they certainly won't meet it," Raine continued, "with whispers and innuendo that maybe Adam Harper had something to do with his death. This is a court of law, ladies and gentlemen. Whispers and innuendos get people punished for things they didn't do. Courts exist to prevent whispers and innuendo from deciding who's right and who's wrong. And frankly, it is insulting not just to Adam, but to you and the entire justice system, to suggest anything decided in this courtroom should be done based on anything other than the evidence, the law, and the burden of proof."

Another pause, to let his righteous indignation settle in with the jurors.

"So what really happened? And why did Mr. Chapman hurry past the most important fact in this case, hoping you wouldn't notice it? I know why he did it, given the rest of his argument, but I hope some of you caught it. Do you remember all of his talk about family and chosen family and choosing to leave the family and choosing to cut off family?"

Only one juror actually nodded in response, but that meant Raine had at least that juror on his side already.

"Mr. Chapman tried to tell you a nice clean story about a father and a son choosing to cut each other off," Raine said, "but that isn't what he described. What he described was a son who was concerned about the welfare of the business his father had built, and a father who was upset by this, but"— Raine stepped forward and punctuated each word with a downward stroke of his hand—"still did not write him out of his will."

Raine took a beat, then repeated, "William Harper did not write Adam Harper out of his will. What he did do was rearrange the order in which the family business would pass to his sons, but he made a point of keeping Adam in the will, albeit conditionally. No matter how mad William Harper was, he still wasn't willing to let Harper Development pass outside of the family so long as one of his sons was alive. That is an uncontroverted and incontrovertible fact."

Raine glanced back at Chapman as he coopted his phrase.

"And do you know what else is uncontroverted and incontrovertible? That William Harper did not put anywhere in his will anything at all about his daughter-in-law inheriting any of the family business. He could have. He did not. Because you can choose family all you want, and that family can choose other people to add to the family, but when it came right down to it, even after Adam tried to take the company away from him, William Harper still wanted the company to stay in his family, his blood family, if at all possible.

"And that's what happened. And Mr. Chapman will never be able to prove otherwise because it simply isn't true."

Raine smiled internally. He was pleased with his presentation. He was also almost finished. Opening statement was supposed to be about the facts, not the law. The law was for closing argument. But he couldn't sit down without telling the jury what the law of the case was and why it mattered to them.

"Mr. Chapman took a moment to rage against the settled law when it comes to how long a person needs to survive in order to inherit. He suggested that it was unfair or unjust. But of course, it's neither. It's the law, and it's the law for a reason. Does it impact Sarah Harper? You might think so, but I'm going to suggest to you that it doesn't. Not any more than the winning lottery numbers impact me if I don't buy a ticket. The law was never going to let the company pass to Sarah. It never did pass. This isn't a situation where she inherited the company and then Adam came and took it back somehow, like a ball on a playground.

"And all you have to do to make sure the law is followed, and Harper Development goes to Adam, who was listed in the will, instead of Sarah, who was not, is... nothing. You don't have to do anything. Mr. Chapman, he's the one who has to do everything. He's the one who has to put on evidence and try to meet the burden of proof and attempt to convince you that you should ignore the law. But he won't be able to do that. And so at the end of the trial, just say as much in your verdict. Find for the defendant, Adam Harper, and let the law play out the way it is intended. Because at the end of the day, that's what William Harper wanted. And that's what justice demands.

Thank you." Raine turned and walked crisply back to his seat.

Adam wrote "Great job!" on his notepad.

Raine allowed himself one visible nod, again with the jurors in mind. He didn't mind if they saw him satisfied with his argument, but he didn't want to appear overconfident. The real work was about to begin.

## 28

J udge Fairfax peered down from the bench. "Mr. Chapman, you may call your first witness."

Chapman stood and announced, "We call Sarah Harper to the stand."

It made sense to call her as the first witness, Raine thought. Their entire case was about Sarah and what she felt she was entitled to. If she was a good witness, then the rest of their case could be built on her testimony. And if she did a poor job, well, they had time to try to bolster her claims through other witnesses. Raine approved of the strategy. In part because it would also allow him to cross-examine her right away. The jury was going to love that drama.

Chapman motioned for Sarah to step up to the judge to be sworn in.

Sarah was dressed in a well-tailored black suit, with her hair up in a bun, and a single pearl necklace around her throat. She looked very respectable. Exactly what the jury would want.

Judge Fairfax stood up and looked down at Sarah. The

judge raised her right hand and instructed Sarah to do the same. "Do you solemnly swear or affirm that the testimony you provide will be the truth, the whole truth, and nothing but the truth?"

"I do," Sarah answered.

The judge then instructed her to take a seat in the witness stand, connected to the side of the judicial bench, between the judge and the jury box.

Chapman took up a spot at the counter that ran all the way around the judge's bench, and began his questioning. "Please state your name for the record."

"Sarah Elizabeth Harper," she answered.

"Could you please explain how you are related to Mark Harper, William Harper, and Adam Harper?" Chapman asked next.

This was all information that everyone already knew, especially after the lawyers' opening statements, but it wasn't evidence unless a witness said it under oath.

"Mark Harper was my husband," Sarah answered. "William Harper was Mark's father and my father-in-law. And Adam was Mark's brother, and I guess he's still my brother-in-law? I'm not sure."

"Of course, of course," Chapman reassured his client. "Let's talk a little bit about Mark, shall we?"

Sarah nodded and smiled sadly. "I'd like that."

She wasn't crying yet, but Raine knew it was coming.

Chapman led her through her relationship with Mark. How they met, their first date, how he proposed—at the top of the Space Needle after buying out the entire restaurant so they had it all to themselves—their wedding, the whole happily-ever-after. Raine had only met them that one time at the beginning of Adam's original lawsuit, and they hadn't seemed all that happy to him.

Chapman confirmed how long they were married and that they never had kids, then moved on to the next topic. "Would you say that Mark was very involved in Harper Development?"

Raine could have objected to the question. It was the definition of a leading question, which was not permissible with your own witness. But he knew he would look petty to the jurors, and he wasn't afraid of the answer that was coming.

"Oh yes," Sarah replied, of course. "He was very involved."

"Even in the day-to-day operations?" Chapman asked.

"Especially the day-to-day operations," Sarah answered. "And also the big-picture stuff. The kind of things his father had always been in charge of. Mark was really moving into a role of helping his father guide the company into the future."

Raine didn't believe that at all, but then he had the advantage of having observed both Bill and Mark Harper. Mark Harper was not someone confident enough to have a vision for the future, and Bill Harper knew that. The jurors wouldn't know any of that.

"Were you aware of your father-in-law's intent to leave the business to Mark in his will?"

Sarah shook her head. "Bill—everyone called him Bill— Bill never talked about that sort of thing. I mean, it was understood that eventually Bill would step down and his sons would take over, but there had never been anything specific laid out. And I certainly didn't know anything about his will."

"Did Mark?"

"I don't think so."

"What about Adam?"

Again, Raine could have objected. "Lack of personal knowledge." Sarah didn't know whether Adam knew. But any objection would look like he was trying to hide the prospective answer, and the information was going to come in anyway when Chapman called Adam to the stand. It wasn't a criminal case; Adam didn't have the right to remain silent or refuse to testify. If a prosecutor so much as suggested to a jury that the defendant should testify, it would be a mistrial and perhaps even a dismissal. In a civil case, it would almost be malpractice not to call the other side to the witness stand. So Raine let the question pass without objection.

"I, I don't know," Sarah answered, honestly even. "I don't know what he knew about Bill's new will, or when he found out. I mean, eventually we all found out, right?" She laughed nervously. "That's why we're here."

Chapman nodded. "That is why we're here."

Raine thought they were there because Sarah didn't like what was in that new will, but he would have to wait his turn to make that point.

"Did Mark have a will?" Chapman asked Sarah next.

"Yes, he did."

"And do you know the contents of that will?"

"Yes," Sarah answered. "We had our wills drafted at the same time. I left everything to him, and he left everything to me."

A typical estate planning setup for a married couple with no children, Raine knew. He'd drafted similar wills for similar couples, although none with the assets the Harpers had.

"So anything he inherited from his father"—Chapman followed the logic—"would have passed on his death to you. Is that how you understand it?"

"Yes," Sarah said. "That's exactly how I understand it."

Chapman took a few minutes then to admit copies of the wills into evidence. Mark Harper's one will and two of Bill Harper's, the one in effect at the time Adam filed his lawsuit and the changed one executed afterward. Admitting the actual documents into evidence would allow witnesses to discuss their provisions freely, and they would also go back to the jury room with the jury during the deliberations. Raine had no problem with any of that—quite the contrary, in fact—and the wills were admitted without objection.

Sarah didn't actually have all that much useful information to provide. As Raine had said in his opening statement, most of the facts were agreed upon. It was a disagreement as to the import of those facts that formed the basis of the case. With the actual wills admitted, Sarah's remaining purpose on the stand was to gain sympathy. She needed the jury to like her, or at least feel sorry for her, if she was to have any chance of winning the company away from Adam. So it was time to cry.

"Let's talk a little about Mark's death," Chapman said gently. "Are you going to be able to do that right now, or do you need a break?"

Sarah provided a preemptive sniffle. "I think I can go on."

Raine didn't roll his eyes. For one thing, the jury would have hated it. For another, he wasn't going to pretend that Sarah wasn't entitled to feel sad about the death of her husband. As an advocate, he had no choice but to endure it and hope that it didn't sway the jury from their path. The judge would instruct them at the end of the trial, before they began their deliberations, that they must allow neither sympathy nor prejudice to affect their verdict, but the reason that was a standard instruction every judge read to every jury was that they were very likely to do exactly that.

"How did Mark die?" Chapman asked.

Sarah's shoulders slumped, almost as if she couldn't believe it himself. "He fell from the nineteenth floor of Harper Tower, the new skyscraper they were building downtown. I still can't believe it."

"Did he jump on his own?" Chapman asked.

Sarah's eyes flashed. "It was not suicide! Mark did not kill himself."

"So it was an accident?" Chapman followed up.

Now it was time to object, before Sarah said what Chapman was leading her to say, namely that Adam might have murdered Mark. For all Raine knew, he might well have. But Sarah shouldn't be allowed to speculate.

"Objection, Your Honor." Raine stood up to address the Court. "Calls for speculation. This witness lacks the personal knowledge to give an opinion as to the manner of death."

"Any response, Mr. Chapman?" Judge Fairfax asked before ruling on the objection.

"Well, Your Honor," Chapman answered, "I believe Ms. Harper knows her husband well enough to give an opinion as to how likely it would be for an experienced construction worker like him to simply fall off an unfinished platform."

The judge frowned slightly. "The witness may testify as to any personal knowledge she might have regarding her husband's experience at construction sites similar to the one being discussed here. She can also give an opinion as to how likely she believes it is that her husband fell accidentally. She may not give any opinions beyond that regarding what else might have happened."

Raine frowned. Technically, he had won the objection, but substantively, Chapman had prevailed. Sarah wouldn't be able to say she thought her husband was murdered, but she wouldn't have to. The jury would understand the implication.

So that was exactly what she did. She swore that Mark was the most experienced and safety-conscious man she had ever met, with years and years of experience in and around construction sites just like the one in question. In her opinion, it was very unlikely that Mark just slipped and fell.

"What about your father-in-law?" Chapman followed up. "Do you have any opinion about how likely it was that he just slipped and fell?"

Raine rose again. "Same objection, Your Honor. Calls for speculation. Lack of personal knowledge."

"Same response, Your Honor," Chapman said.

"Same ruling," Fairfax declared.

Raine sat down again. At least Sarah wouldn't use the actual phrase "I think he was murdered." She would just strongly suggest it, which she then did.

The good news about the objections and the focus on whether Bill and Mark were murder victims or just fatally clumsy was that Sarah forgot to get emotional about her husband's death. She was too focused on giving an opinion on how it happened. She had testified to everything she had information on and had only managed a sniffle. Raine was going to call that a win.

"No further questions at this time," Chapman announced, and walked toward his seat.

"Any cross-examination, Mr. Raine?" the judge invited.

Raine didn't actually have that much. He had already blocked her from saying the most damaging thing. And she hadn't come across as any more sympathetic than anyone else who had lost a spouse. But the jury would expect Raine to ask at least a few questions. Failing to pose any at all might be interpreted as endorsing her testimony and her claim.

"Yes, Your Honor," Raine answered the judge.

He came out from behind his table and approached the witness stand. He wasn't going to stand in the same spot as Chapman. Chapman had stood in a location of support. Raine was going to stand in a location of confrontation. Directly in front of her and one step too close.

"You thought Mark should be more involved in the day-to-day operation of the business, didn't you?" he challenged her.

Sarah took a moment to think before responding. It was smart to do when being questioned by opposing counsel, but if she kept doing it, she would start to look shady. You didn't have to think about the truth.

"Well, as I said," she hedged, "he was already very involved in the running of the company."

"Very involved?" Raine questioned.

Sarah shifted in her seat. "He was involved."

"And you thought he should be more involved," Raine pressed.

"I thought he could be more involved," Sarah answered. "He was very good at it. They could have used his skills even more than they already were."

"They, meaning his father, correct?" Raine asked her.

She hesitated, then surrendered a nod. "Yes."

"But his father didn't like giving up control, did he?" Raine asked. "Bill Harper was not known for letting other people do his work for him, was he?"

"Mark's father owned that company and could run it however he saw fit," Sarah replied through tight lips.

"And you could have an opinion about how he saw fit to run it and how he involved your husband, isn't that also true?" Raine wasn't going to let her wriggle off the hook.

"I suppose that's true," she allowed.

"And your opinion was that he should have involved Mark more." Raine put it to her again. "Isn't that true, Ms. Harper?"

Sarah sighed, then waved a hand at him. "Fine. Yes. I thought Mark should have been more involved in the running of the company. He had the experience, and he had waited his turn. It was time, in my opinion."

"And you thought that would be to the benefit of the company, correct?" Raine asked.

"Of course," she answered.

"So, then you would agree with me"—Raine took another half step toward the witness stand, to really get into her personal space and make her feel uncomfortable—"that Bill Harper was excluding his sons from the operation of the business to the detriment of the corporation. Isn't that what you're saying, Ms. Harper?"

Sarah frowned. "I'm not sure that's exactly what I'm saying."

Raine took a step back again and crossed his arms. "Somebody probably should have done something about that, huh?"

"If you're talking about Adam's ridiculous lawsuit to steal

the company from his father," Sarah chided, "that was a terrible idea and never would have worked."

"But at least he tried," Raine said. He stepped to her again. "Mark never even tried, did he?"

That same contempt for her weak husband that Raine had seen poorly hidden in her eyes at that first hearing returned. Whatever answer she had got stuck in her throat.

"He never stood up to his father, did he, Ms. Harper?" Raine pushed. "Never."

Chapman finally came to the rescue of his client. "Objection, Your Honor. Counsel is badgering the witness."

"I'm asking her a question, Your Honor," Raine defended. "That's what cross-examination is."

"You can ask it in a different way," Judge Fairfax instructed. "With a different tone."

Raine considered. He didn't really want to. He didn't need to. And now that she'd had a moment to think, Sarah was going to change her answer anyway.

"That's all right, Your Honor," Raine said. "I have no further questions."

He'd made his point. Chapman had as well. The first witness was complete. Raine returned to his seat feeling victorious and awaited Chapman's next witness.

Things turned very dry very quickly. The rest of Chapman's case was less personal and more obscure. The only other family member to call was Adam, and it became clear pretty quickly that Adam was going to be the last witness Chapman called to the stand. Raine approved of that strategy as well. Get the entire rest of the case out so that if Adam argued with any of it, the jury would have the information to disbelieve him. But that meant a parade of lower-level Harper Development employees, to talk about income and assets, outlays and liabilities. He even called a law professor from Seattle University Law School to talk about the history of "common disaster" and the Survival Rule.

Raine made sure to cross-examine each and every witness, although not necessarily at length. There wasn't much Joan from Accounting could say to really hurt his case or bolster Chapman's, but he got the law professor to admit that the one-hundred-and-twenty-hour rule, or some variation on it, existed in all fifty states and England.

It took Chapman several days to put on his case-in-chief. Raine and Adam were there for all of it, talking only minimally and only when Raine couldn't avoid it by rushing to the bathroom on any recess or insisting he needed to check his email.

Sawyer stopped by a few times to see how Raine was doing, but with one exception, he never got to talk to her because by the time the judge took a break, Sawyer had had already left the courtroom again. Sommers stopped by a few times as well. She appeared to be interested in the testimony of some of the more technical financial witnesses, because she would stay for an entire witness's testimony, taking notes, then leave again. Raine asked her if he was missing something that she was seeing, but she said no, she was just taking the opportunity to learn about the inner workings of one of Seattle's largest real estate developers. "Opportunities are either taken or squandered," she told him, "and I don't squander opportunities."

The trial found itself in a Friday afternoon when Chapman announced he had only one more witness to call.

"I'd like to adjourn for the week, Your Honor," Chapman requested. "This last witness will take some time, I believe. We won't finish with his testimony in the time we have left

this afternoon, and I would prefer not to split up his testimony, especially over a weekend."

Judge Fairfax frowned at the clock, but looked down at
Raine. "Any objection to that proposed course of action, Mr.
Raine?"

Raine was tempted to object to any course of action
Chapman proposed, but he would take the opportunity to
prepare Adam a little bit more before he testified. "No objection, Your Honor."

"Then court is adjourned until nine a.m. Monday morning," the judge declared. She banged her gavel and departed
to the bailiff's call to rise.

Raine waited for the bailiff to lead the jurors into the jury
room to collect their things and close the jury room door
before addressing his client.

"We should meet over the weekend," Raine said. "He is
going to have you on the stand for hours. We need to be
prepared."

But Adam just shrugged. "I feel good about how things
are going. I don't think we need to meet."

Raine cocked his head at him. "We definitely need to
meet. I'm your lawyer, and I'm telling you we need to meet."

"That's funny"—Adam tapped Raine on the chest—
"because I'm the client, and I say we don't. And the client is
always right. What you say is just advice. What I say goes."

Raine pursed his lips. "You're right. I can't force you to
meet with me. I can just tell you it's stupid not to."

"Noted." Adam handed his notepad to Raine, who took it
along with the pen he had lent Adam. "See you Monday."

Adam exited the courtroom, and Raine was left with a
mix of emotions. Frustration at his client—that was nothing

new—but some relief that he might have at least some part of his weekend free.

"You want me to say hi to Nat for you?" Chapman came up behind Raine to ask.

It took all Raine had not to throw an elbow into that smarmy smile he knew was on Chapman's face.

"I couldn't care less what you do this weekend, Chapman." Raine turned around slowly to stare down his opponent. They were the only two left in the courtroom. "I'll be doing everything I can to make sure you lose this case."

Chapman didn't reply, but the slight twitch at the corner of his eye made Raine think there was a chance Chapman might cancel whatever plans he had with Natalie to try to put even more work in than Raine. That wouldn't be as hard as Raine was making it seem. As soon as he got outside, he was calling his favorite restaurant and making dinner reservations for two. It was his weekend with the boys, but Jason would just have to babysit his little brother. Raine needed to see Sawyer.

## 29

L a Belle Epoch was not Raine's favorite restaurant, but it was the one Sawyer had wanted to go to when he called to ask her out. So he canceled the reservations he'd made at the steak and seafood joint on the waterfront and instead reserved a table for two at the French restaurant at the top of one of the office towers in the financial district. At least there was parking. And Sawyer.

The restaurant was just a little fancier than Raine was used to. He'd never made enough money to be able to spend it without thinking. La Belle Epoch was four and a half stars for food, but a solid five dollar signs for cost. Sawyer was going to insist on paying for her own food, but it still pained Raine to order an entrée that cost more than two full meals, with drinks, at any of the places he normally ate. But such was the price of love. Or at least the early stage of dating.

The reservation was for Saturday night. Friday was already booked, and Raine was wiped out anyway from the week of trial. He spent Friday afternoon returning calls on all of his other cases and checking in with Sommers. She had called ostensibly to see how the trial was going, but Raine knew it was really to see if any other useful witnesses would be discussing her particular game of inside baseball.

The Saturday night crowd was even more opulent than he had expected. There was a lot of money in Seattle, although most of it had managed to avoid Raine over the years. Still, the restaurant was packed with people whose clothes and attitudes communicated that they spent money without thinking. Raine supposed that was why the prices were what they were.

"Why did you want to come here, again?" he asked Sawyer after they had been seated. "The food?"

"Oh, no." Sawyer laughed over the frenetic buzz of the restaurant. "Food is food. I want to people watch. I heard this is the place to see anyone in this town worth seeing."

"Well, you're definitely worth seeing tonight." Raine knew how to take an opportunity too. "You look stunning."

She did too. She wore a long evening dress, with a slit halfway up her thigh, stilettos that made her taller than Raine, and dangling earrings that brushed the tops of her shoulders.

"Flatterer." Sawyer laughed. "But thanks. I figured I should dress up a little, and a necktie just wouldn't have gone with this dress."

Raine thought if anyone could have pulled that off, it was her, but he demurred. Instead he reached for the glass of wine and raised it to his companion. "To a quiet evening, without death or near-death experiences."

But Sawyer grimaced and looked around nervously. "I think you just jinxed it. Someone here is going to die now. Nice job."

Raine looked around as well to see who the likely victim

might be. Then he saw someone who surprised him. Two someones, in fact.

"Huh, would you look at that," he said with a nod toward the far corner of the restaurant.

"Look at what?" Sawyer turned around to see what Raine was indicating.

"More of a who, I suppose," Raine said.

"Whom," Sawyer corrected. "Since we're looking at them."

"Okay, would you look at whom," Raine said, then shook his head. "No, that's not right."

"What or whom am I looking at?" Sawyer asked, scanning the crowd.

"My client, Adam Harper," Raine answered, "and my opponent, Sarah Harper."

Sawyer took a moment, then spotted them. "I didn't get a great look at them in court," she admitted. "I didn't really care about them. Is that them near that giant potted-fern thing?"

"Yep, that's them," Raine confirmed. He took a long sip of wine.

"I wonder what they're doing here," Sawyer said, turning back to face Raine.

"I wonder what they're doing here together," Raine added. "I told Adam we needed to meet this weekend. He refused. Maybe this is why."

"Do you think there's something funny going on?" Sawyer asked. "Maybe they're having a secret affair?"

"It's weird to sue your lover," Raine remarked.

Sawyer chuckled. "Did you really just say 'lover'?"

Raine shrugged. "It seemed like the most accurate word, given the context."

"How very lawyerly of you," Sawyer responded. "Don't ever use that word in front of me again."

Raine agreed, then returned to his suppositions. "This isn't good. Whatever it is, it isn't good."

"Why not?" Sawyer questioned. "I mean, they are related. Or they were. Maybe they're just catching up or trying to work through the problem on their own."

"Without their lawyers?" Raine wondered.

"Sometimes lawyers can get in the way," Sawyer said. "Lawyers in the room means the stakes are high and blood pressures are up. Lawyers leave the room, people can just be people again."

"We are in the middle of trial," Raine said. "Literally the middle. Chapman is going to call Adam as his last witness, then rest, and then it'll be my turn. If this case could have been settled, it would have by now. No, this is something else."

"Something nefarious?" Sawyer suggested.

"Yes." Raine grinned. "Nefarious."

"So what is it, then?" Sawyer pressed.

Raine thought for a moment. "I'm not sure. But this is a romantic restaurant, and it's not unheard of for a woman to fall in love with her husband's brother."

"Or a man to fall in love with his brother's wife," Sawyer added.

"Exactly." Raine considered for a moment. "Is this whole lawsuit just a ruse? A red herring to throw people off the scent? Did Adam and Sarah murder Bill and Mark together?"

"That's a big jump from one dinner, Dan," Sawyer warned. She glanced over at them again. "Oh, they're kissing. They're kissing."

Raine looked over again at Adam and Sarah. It looked like they might be kissing, but Raine and Sawyer were too far away to be sure. And that giant fern thing was blocking part of the view.

"And now they're leaving," Raine observed.

"Probably taking the evening somewhere more private," Sawyer posited. "Speaking of which..." She reached a hand across the table to take a hold of Raine's. "Any chance we can go back to your apartment tonight? I never did get to see it the night you almost drowned in Lake Washington."

Raine was watching Adam and Sarah intently. "What? Oh, uh, no. No, my boys are with me this weekend. I need to go straight back there after dinner, actually."

Sawyer let go of his hand and raised an eyebrow. "Are you kidding me?"

"I mean"—he hesitated—"we could probably do something quick."

Sawyer took a moment, then smiled at him. "I don't want quick. Not the first time. I want to savor it. Make it something to remember."

"Something to build on?" Raine suggested, but then immediately regretted it.

"Don't get too far ahead of yourself, Dan," she cautioned. "Let's take a tour of the first floor before we start talking about buying the whole building."

Raine let Sawyer's words sink into his brain. "You're right." He nodded several times, although more to himself than to her. "You're exactly right."

## 30

Monday morning arrived, and Raine was still debating whether he should confront Adam about his dinner date with their opponent. He walked into the courtroom his customary fifteen minutes before court started, but Adam wasn't there. Neither was Sarah. Chapman was, though.

Raine made his way to his counsel table, making no effort to engage with Chapman. To his considerable surprise, Chapman made no effort to talk to him either. Raine stole a glance and saw that Chapman was staring intently at his laptop screen, his fingers flying fervently across the keyboard. He looked like a student whose paper was due in about ten seconds.

The door to the courtroom opened, and in walked Sarah Harper. Raine was prohibited by the lawyer ethics rules from speaking with a represented person, especially an opposing party, so it was easy for him not to say hello to her as she passed and sat down next to her lawyer, who ignored her as well as he tried to finish whatever he was working on.

One minute later, the courtroom door opened again, and Adam walked in. His usual dopey grin was missing, but there was a different kind of confidence in his expression. It didn't seem to have its origins in blissful ignorance. Just the opposite, really. He looked like he knew something. Raine wanted to know too.

"Good morning, Adam," he greeted his client. "Do you have anything you want to tell your lawyer before we start up this trial again? This trial that will determine the future of your father's multimillion-dollar company? Anything? Anything at all?"

Adam thought for a moment, then shook his head. "No, there's nothing I want to tell you."

They all sat in awkward silence until the bailiff came out and announced the judge's arrival.

"All rise! The King County Superior Court is now in session, the Honorable Veronica Fairfax presiding!"

It was exactly 9:00 a.m. The judge was still running the courtroom on a fast track. "Are we ready for the jury?" she asked the lawyers.

Raine looked at his client, giving him one last chance to tell him whatever he wasn't telling him, but Adam just shrugged at him. Raine sighed, then looked up to the judge. "The defense is ready."

Answering first reminded Raine that Chapman should have answered first. All eyes turned to Chapman, and he finally pulled himself away from his laptop. He pushed himself to his feet. "Yes, sorry, Your Honor. The plaintiff is ready as well. We are ready, yes."

"Bring in the jury," Fairfax instructed her bailiff, and the bailiff immediately set to the task.

A few minutes later, the jury had emerged from the jury

room and was seated in the jury box. Raine and everyone else had stood for their entrance. He sat down again and awaited Chapman's announcement that he was calling Adam Harper to the stand.

"Does the plaintiff have any further witnesses?" Judge Fairfax inquired formally.

"Yes, Your Honor," Chapman answered. "The plaintiff calls Robert Perez to the stand."

Raine's head jerked to look at Chapman, then Sarah, then back at Adam.

Who the hell was Robert Perez?

Robert Perez, it turned out, was that witness Chapman had alluded to in his opening statement, the one who would have an opinion regarding exactly how Bill and Mark Harper died. He was a retired medical examiner from Oregon, making some money on the side consulting. Raine recalled seeing his name on the witness list and looking him up online, but Chapman had never provided any sort of expert report. When Chapman had announced the previous Friday that he only had one more witness to go and he hadn't called Adam yet, Raine just assumed they weren't going to hear from retired Dr. Robert Perez after all.

Raine was surprised by the turn of events, but he wasn't unprepared. He was ready to shred the good doctor, starting with the fact that he had never actually examined either body and was relying solely on the autopsy reports prepared by the King County Medical Examiner who was noticeably absent from the proceedings.

Speaking of absent from the proceedings, Raine took a moment to scan the courtroom. Detective Kavendish had said he was going to come and watch Adam's testimony. Had he been tipped off that Chapman wouldn't be calling Adam after all? How deep did the conspiracy go?

Raine shook his head slightly to bring his focus back to the task at hand. Paying close attention during Chapman's direct exam, then springing from his seat, predator-like, to dismantle whatever theories Perez had tried to establish.

For his part, Chapman seemed even more distracted. He fetched Perez from where he had been waiting in the hallway, then returned to his laptop as Judge Fairfax swore him in.

Dr. Perez sat on the witness stand, and Raine expected Chapman to step out into the well, but instead Chapman posed his first question from behind the table. Raine was stunned. One of the most basic rules of effective trial advocacy was never to examine your witnesses from your seat. Take the room. Own the room. Don't recoil from it.

"Could you please state your name for the record," Chapman said, eyes on his laptop.

"Robert Perez." A professional witness, he turned to deliver his answer to the jurors. Jurors loved that.

"And how are you employed, sir?" Chapman asked, seemingly without having to think about it.

"I am a retired forensic pathologist," Perez answered. "I worked for the State of Oregon for thirty-two years. Now I own my own consulting business."

"What sort of things do you consult on?" Chapman was asking the questions almost before his witness could answer.

"I review forensic pathology examinations," Perez told the jurors, "things like autopsies, and provide my opinion as to the accuracy and reliability of the results reported in those reports."

"Did you do any such consulting on this case?" Chapman finally raised his face to look at his witness.

Perez turned to the jury again. "I did," he reported.

"Uh, what were the names of the people whose autopsy reports you reviewed?" Chapman asked. He wasn't looking at his laptop anymore, but he was still standing behind his table, essentially at the edge of the proceedings, about as far away from the jurors as he could be.

"William Harper and Mark Harper, I believe," Perez answered with a slight grin.

"Yes, correct," Chapman said. "And, um, did you review those reports?"

Perez confirmed the question. "Yes. As I said, I reviewed the autopsy reports for a William Harper and a Mark Harper. I'm guessing they're related."

Chapman didn't respond. He was leaning down, whispering to his client.

Everyone in the courtroom waited to see what would happen next. It was all very uneven.

Finally, Chapman stood up again. "Uh, thank you, Doctor. No further questions."

Raine's eyebrows shot up. He looked at his client, but Adam seemed to have no reaction whatsoever to what was going on around him.

Judge Fairfax seemed taken aback, however, just like Raine. It took her a moment before she leaned forward and asked, "Any cross-examination, Mr. Raine?"

Raine wasn't sure what to do. He had asked at least one question to every single witness up to that point. But Dr. Perez hadn't said anything damaging. He hadn't really said anything at all. If Raine asked a question, not only might the doctor try to use it to tell the jury about his findings, which he was undoubtedly dying to share—that was why he had taken the case and shown up to testify. It also meant Chapman could ask more questions, and there was a chance that he would shake whatever was distracting him long enough to do a decent examination of Perez and extract the information he had forgotten to the first time through.

On the other hand, if Raine didn't ask any questions, Perez couldn't say anything, and Chapman would be prohibited from asking any more questions himself. There was a risk some of the jurors might punish Raine for avoiding engagement with the opposing side's expert, but they were probably trying to figure out what was going on as well.

"No, Your Honor," Raine answered. "No questions for this witness."

Judge Fairfax frowned at the lawyers—a frown of puzzlement, not displeasure—and excused a likewise puzzled Dr. Perez from the witness stand.

"Does the plaintiff have any further witnesses?" Judge Fairfax asked Chapman.

Chapman looked to Sarah. Sarah shook her head. And Chapman answered the judge's question. "No, Your Honor. The plaintiff rests."

Raine wondered what had just happened, but he seemed to be the only one at either counsel table who didn't know. He didn't like that feeling.

"Mr. Raine," the judge interrupted his thoughts, "are you prepared to call witnesses now, or shall we adjourn? I don't believe you were expecting to put on your case quite this soon."

"Uh, that's correct, Your Honor," Raine answered. "I believe the expectation was that the soonest I would start calling witnesses was tomorrow. Could we possibly adjourn until then? I'd like the opportunity to marshal my witnesses."

What he really wanted was an opportunity to ask his client what the hell was going on. Why hadn't Chapman called Adam to the stand? Why had he called a pathologist only to not ask him his opinion as to the deaths of Bill and Mark Harper? And what did all of it have to do with Adam and Sarah's weekend rendezvous?

Judge Fairfax was willing to give Raine some time, but she wasn't willing to waste an entire court day. "We will adjourn for the morning," she announced, "but we will reconvene after lunch. Everyone should be assembled in the courtroom no later than one o'clock this afternoon."

She banged her gavel and retreated to her chambers. The bailiff called out her departure, then escorted the jurors into the jury room.

When the door closed, Raine pointed at Adam. "Okay, now we need to meet. You're taking the stand at one o'clock. I'll be asking the questions. We need to prepare."

Adam stood up and stretched. "I think I can answer questions without preparing. It's not a math test."

"No, it's way more important than a math test," Raine scolded. "The entire case, the fate of your father's company, could very well be determined by how well your testimony goes this afternoon."

Adam looked at Raine for several seconds, then reached out and placed a hand on his shoulder. "I want you to know that I really do appreciate how hard you've worked on this case. I'll see you at one o'clock." With that, he turned and walked out of the courtroom.

Raine was beside himself. He turned to see what Chapman thought of what was going on, but he was huddled in his own secret whisper consultation with his client. He didn't look happy, though, from what Raine could tell.

Raine sighed. He had a few hours to prepare himself for the direct examination of his client. He couldn't make Adam prepare, but that just made it all the more important that he did. He'd grab a coffee at the café, then find a cubicle in the courthouse law library. That way he wouldn't waste time traveling back and forth to his office. It had been a morning of surprises. He wanted his afternoon to be surprise-free.

He would be disappointed.

## 31

When Raine returned to Judge Fairfax's courtroom at 12:55, Adam and Sarah were already there. He noted that because they were standing next to each other. Chapman was also there. Raine noted that because when he walked up to the three of them, Chapman handed him a document.

"This is your copy of a proposed settlement agreement," Chapman informed him. "Our clients appear to have reached an amicable resolution of the case."

"Settlement agreement?" Raine had expected the afternoon to go in directions he hadn't anticipated, but he never saw a settlement agreement coming. He looked down at the lengthy document, heavy in his hand. "What's the agreement?"

"We're going to dissolve the company," Adam explained.

"And split the proceeds fifty-fifty," Sarah added.

"Dissolve the company?" Raine repeated. "You're going to dissolve the company your father built from the ground up, while it's in the middle of building a luxury skyscraper in the center of downtown Seattle?"

"Yes," Adam answered sternly. "That's what we're going to do."

"Did you know about this?" Raine demanded of Chapman. "Is that why you were so weird this morning?"

"I can't divulge client communications, obviously," Chapman answered, "but I can confirm that I was distracted this morning, and I drafted this between the time court adjourned this morning and now."

"Unbelievable." Raine threw his hands up. "How many weeks of trial did we waste?" He pointed at Adam. "You're paying for every minute of it too. Especially if you manage to dissolve a company worth more than most small countries."

"What do you mean if we manage to do it?" Adam asked. "It's an agreement. We signed it. That's that."

"That is most definitely not that," Raine responded. "Your father's will was already in probate when this lawsuit got filed. You'll need the judge's permission to do anything to the assets. Furthermore, this case is halfway to a verdict. You can't just dismiss a case once the trial has started. You make a motion to dismiss the case, and then the judge can grant or deny it. They always grant it, but I don't know. This judge? This case? This proposed settlement? She might not grant that motion to dismiss. There's a lot more to this than you two lovebirds signing something over lunch."

"Lovebirds?" Adam barked.

"What do you mean lovebirds?" Sarah demanded.

"You know what? We don't have time for this." Raine threw the agreement onto the table. "The judge is going to be out any sec—"

"All rise!" shouted the bailiff. "The King County Superior

Court is now in session, the Honorable Veronica Fairfax presiding!"

Judge Fairfax emerged to take her seat above the litigants and bid them to sit down. Then she asked, "Are you prepared to call your first witness, Mr. Raine?"

Raine stood up again. "Apparently, I am not, Your Honor."

Fairfax frowned. "What is that supposed to mean?"

Chapman stood and held up the document in his hand. "The parties have reached a resolution, Your Honor. We have prepared a settlement agreement that addresses all of the issues in the litigation."

"A settlement agreement?" Fairfax asked. "What's the agreement?"

"That's what I asked," Raine couldn't stop himself from putting in.

"Uh, it involves the liquidation of all corporate assets," Chapman explained, "and distributing them equally between the parties."

"You want to dissolve the entire corporation?" Judge Fairfax asked. "Wouldn't that impact hundreds maybe even thousands of employees? What about the corporation's outstanding business contracts? What about the current construction project? What will happen to that?"

"Those are issues to be worked out in further negotiations." Chapman tried to assuage the Court's concerns. "What matters today is that this agreement effectively terminates this lawsuit. The trial is over."

"I will say whether this lawsuit is terminated," Judge Fairfax replied sharply. "I will decide when this trial is over."

Raine nodded along with the judge's rebuke.

"Mr. Raine, have you had a chance to review this proposed settlement agreement?" the judge asked.

"I have not, Your Honor," he answered. "I was first advised of it when I walked into the courtroom just before Your Honor took the bench."

"If I may, Your Honor"—Adam spoke up—"I don't need Mr. Raine to review the document. If he doesn't agree with it, then I will just fire him."

Judge Fairfax had made a promise that if Adam spoke out of turn, even one word, then he and Raine both would get thirty days in jail for contempt of court. But things had changed significantly in the last few minutes.

The judge took a deep breath, then addressed everyone as calmly and evenly as she ever had. "Thank you, Mr. Harper. I should advise you that once a trial has started, a lawyer may not withdraw from a case without the Court's permission. Therefore, for the purposes of this case, and this proposed settlement, Mr. Raine remains your lawyer until I say otherwise."

Raine wasn't any happier about that arrangement than Adam obviously was, but they both kept their mouths shut.

"Allow me to say that I am not opposed to a mid-trial settlement in the abstract," the judge continued. "To the contrary, it has been my experience that the pressures of trial often help litigants reassess the relative strengths and weaknesses of their positions. However, from what very little I have heard about the proposed settlement, I have some questions that I will need answered before I allow this case to be dismissed and William Harper's will removed from probate. Therefore, I am going to adjourn this case one more time, until tomorrow morning at nine, to give myself and Mr. Raine the opportunity to review the proposed settlement in detail. Perhaps, after doing so, the Court's concerns will be allayed. If so, I will happily thank and excuse our jurors and bring this case to a close."

Raine looked around at the others. Adam and Sarah didn't look happy, but they seemed resigned. Chapman was just standing there, as if in shock.

"I would ask if there are any questions," the judge said, "but I want to wait to take any questions until tomorrow morning. Court is adjourned."

Adam and Sarah made a beeline for the door as soon as the gavel hit the strike plate. Chapman started packing up his things. Raine just wanted to get out of there too. When he turned toward the exit, he was met by Sommers, who was standing at the first row of seats.

"What the hell just happened?" she asked.

Raine shook his head. "I'm not sure."

"That's okay," Sommers said. "We've got a bigger problem anyway."

## 32

Sommers took Raine back to his office, where he had a guest waiting. Emily Park. And did she have some information for him!

"We figured it out," Sommers told Raine once the three of them were seated in the conference room. "Well, Emily figured it out. But she told me. And now we're telling you."

"Figured what out?" Raine asked. "What are you telling me?"

"We're telling you," Emily said, "what your client was really doing with the Harper Tower and why he really wanted to get control of his father's company."

Emily Park was in her early sixties, with naturally silver hair and sharp eyes. Her voice was deep and melodic. Sommers had said she knew everyone and everything in their industry. Raine could believe it.

Raine found himself relieved to hear that Adam was in fact up to something. Adam had been acting so suspicious for so long. He didn't want to believe he had imagined it all. "What was he doing?"

"He was overselling the deposits," Sommers answered, "and pocketing the money for himself."

"It took us a while to figure it out," Emily said. "There were a lot of different agents who had negotiated deposits for their clients, but none of them had done so many themselves that they became suspicious. It was only after you spoke with Deborah and Ethan at the award banquet that people started talking with each other, and we realized just how many deposits had been presold. Too many."

"And then I listened to the testimony of all of the financial officers at Harper," Sommers said. "None of them said anything about any deposit money. He diverted it all away somewhere."

"He's already sold more deposits than the building will have units," Emily added.

"He can't let Harper Tower be completed," Sommers said. "His fraud will be exposed. That's the real reason he sued his dad to take over the company."

"And when it looked like that wasn't going to work..." Raine realized.

"He killed him." Sommers finished his sentence.

"And then I told him about his dad's new will," Raine remembered, "and the Survival Rule."

"And so he killed his brother too," Sommers said. "Just in time."

Raine shook his head. "Wait. Wait. This is all conjecture at this point. I mean not the oversold deposits, not the fraud. Hell, he's about to dissolve the entire company, leaving everyone holding the bag. But the murder stuff. We don't know that. We can't prove that."

The three of them sat in silence for several moments.

Then Sommers spoke up. "Get him to confess," she said.

"Confess to murder?" Raine questioned. "How?"

"You're the only person he would confess to," Sommers said. "You're his lawyer. You can't tell anyone."

"So what good is a confession?" Raine questioned.

"What if someone else overhears it?" Emily asked. "Someone who's not a lawyer."

"Someone who didn't work on the case with you," Sommers added.

"You want me to trick my own client into confessing to me, but have a secret eavesdropper who can go to the cops?" Raine asked.

"Yes," Sommers answered.

"No," Raine said. "I can't do that. I'd lose my license, and rightfully so."

"Damn it," Sommers hissed.

"No, don't worry," Raine consoled. "I have an idea."

"What?" Sommers asked.

Raine took out his phone. "I'm going to arrange a meeting with him and Sarah."

"Sarah?" Sommers questioned. "Isn't she your opponent?"

"Technically, yes," Raine answered, "which is even better. Adam can bring his own eavesdropper to the meeting. Anything he says won't be privileged because of her presence, and it'll be his fault. She's about to go into business with him. I think she'd want to know he's a murderer."

Raine dialed Adam's number, but of course there was no answer. So Raine sent a text.

> We need to meet. Tonight. I know about the deposits. The settlement agreement will expose those. We need to fix it and sign a new one. Everyone.

Adam replied almost immediately:

> 9:00. Harper Tower. Gate will be open.

Raine frowned.

> My office?

But Adam was firm.

> I'm working tonight. Harper Tower. 9:00. Bring the new agreement.

Raine rubbed a hand over his mouth, then agreed.

> Sounds good. See you then.

"Is it set?" Sommers asked. "Are you meeting him?"

"Yep," Raine confirmed. "Nine o'clock. Harper Tower."

"Where he killed the other two people?" Emily questioned.

Raine nodded, then grinned at her. "Aren't you glad you don't have to be there?"

"Well, I'm coming," Sommers announced.

Raine's smile broadened. He knew she'd have his back.

A dam was good to his word. The gate was open. And there was no sign or sound of guard dogs.

"Are you ready?" Raine asked Sommers.

"Ready enough," Sommers answered. "Hopefully it goes fast. They're both in the office trailer. You rattle him with the details about the deposit fraud. He says something incriminating about either or both deaths. Sarah hears it and realizes she can't go into business with a murderer. With three of us there, he doesn't dare try anything, then I take Sarah to the police, and you draft up a fee agreement to defend him against two counts of murder in the first degree. Win-win-win. Well, win-win-win-lose, but he's the one who loses."

"You make it sound so easy," Raine remarked.

"Visualize easy," she told him. "Not everything is as complicated as you lawyers try to make it."

But it was never easy.

"Oh my God." Raine pointed to the black sedan parked just up the street from the open gate.

"What?" Sommers looked in the direction he was pointing, but she didn't know what he was indicating specifically.

"That car," Raine said. "That's the car that tried to run me off the road."

"Are you sure?" Sommers asked. "It looks like every other black luxury sedan."

"There's one way to tell." He was already halfway to the car. When Sommers caught up to him, he pointed to the damage to the vehicle's right rear quarter panel. "Yes," Raine said. "I'm sure."

Sommers covered her mouth and looked back at the gate they were about to go through. "This must be Adam's car. Adam tried to kill you."

Raine nodded. That changed everything. They were still going to do the plan. It was even more important to get the evidence necessary to get Adam into custody. But it meant Adam was even more dangerous than they had thought.

They walked back, and Raine pushed the gate open with a jangle and a creak. Raine went inside first. Sommers followed right behind, pulling the gate to behind her. It was dark inside. Darker than Raine remembered from his previous visits. He could make out the trailer, but there were no lights on inside.

"Where is he?" Sommers asked in a hushed voice.

Raine shook his head. "I don't know. It's nine. He said he'd be here."

After a few more moments, their eyes adjusted to the darkness, and Raine could make out a faint light up ahead near the construction elevator they had seen last time they had been sneaking around the site in the dark. Raine tugged on Sommers's sleeve, and they made their way over.

The light was coming from inside the elevator car, which

was stopped on the ground floor. Resting on the pavement in front of it was an access card with a sticky note on it. Raine picked it up so they could both read the note:

*I'm working on Floor 19. Use card and come up.*

"Well, that sounds like a terrible idea," Sommers commented.

Raine could hardly disagree. "Do we just leave? I can ask to withdraw in the morning, and we walk away from everything else."

Sommers put her fists on her hips and frowned at him. "J. Daniel Raine, are you the sort of person who walks away from things?"

Raine allowed the slightest grin. "I hope not."

"I hope not too," Sommers replied. "Because I'm not about to work for a person who walks away from things."

Raine found the sensor for the card and flashed it. The grating that functioned as a door for the elevator opened, and they stepped inside. Raine flashed the card again at the control panel and pressed the button marked "19".

"Here we go," he said.

"Watch your step," Sommers quipped. "It's a long way down."

The ride was rough and rickety. The elevator rose on a track that was bolted to the outside of the building. It wasn't made for comfort. It barely seemed made for safety. But when they reached the nineteenth floor, the grating opened, and they stepped off onto a floor that was actually more finished than Raine had expected.

Raine had imagined a network of steel girders with little to nothing in between, leaving them to walk along the girders like balance beams. Instead, there were no exposed girders, or exposed anything for that matter. No pipes sticking out or wires hanging down. Dim lights hung from wires that crisscrossed the ceiling, mostly near the elevators, then with decreasing frequency toward the interior. The only things missing were the interior and exterior walls. The lack of interior walls was visually interesting but not particularly concerning. The lack of exterior walls was what had allowed Bill and Mark Harper to fall to their deaths.

"Let's go to the middle of the floor," Raine suggested.

"Good idea," Sommers agreed.

They made their way carefully toward the center of the building, away from the exposed edges.

"Adam?" Raine called out. "I'm here with the new agreement. Are you and Sarah here?"

There was no answer.

"Adam?"

Then a response. It was Adam's voice, but the strange acoustics of an open floor a hundred feet off the ground made it impossible to determine the direction it came from. "Don't move. I'll be right there."

Adam's instruction not to move made Raine very much want to move from their current spot. They hadn't reached anywhere close to the center of the building. They were approximately twenty feet from the elevator and the exposed side of the structure.

"Look, Adam," Raine called out into the dimly lit emptiness surrounding them. "I know what you did."

"I said don't move!" Adam's voice bounced off the walls.

There was no way Raine was standing still after that. They had a choice. They could go deeper into the building, where there were large swaths of black between the fewer and fewer lights. Adam was likely hiding in one of those unlit pockets. Or they could inch back toward the elevator, where there was more light and an escape route. Raine chose option B and motioned to Sommers to start backing up toward the elevator.

"I know what you did!" Raine repeated. "But I can help. I'm your lawyer." Then, remembering the plan, "Is Sarah here?"

Adam suddenly stepped out of the darkness. He was some thirty feet away. "Did you bring the corrected settlement agreement?"

Raine held up the document he had brought. It was just his copy of the original settlement agreement. But Adam wouldn't know that.

"Is Sarah here?" Raine asked again. The plan wasn't going to work if Sarah didn't hear the murder confession.

"I can get her signature," Adam shouted. He extended an open hand. "Give me the agreement."

Raine waved the document. "Why don't you come here and get it. I don't feel comfortable moving around too much up here."

"This isn't working," Sommers whispered.

"I know," Raine whispered back. "I'm working on it."

"We need to improvise," Sommers said. Then she shouted, "Adam, we know you defrauded all of those investors. You're going to prison unless you have something even bigger you can offer the cops."

"What are you doing?" Raine whisper-yelled.

"Improvising," Sommers answered. "It needs to be really big, Adam!" she shouted again. "You know what I'm talking about, right?"

Adam's face contorted in anger, and he started to march

directly toward them. "Just say it! Say it out loud! I want to hear you say it!"

Adam was closing the gap fast. They were out of time.

"We know you murdered your father and brother, Adam," Raine said as Adam bore down on them, "to cover up the deposit fraud. Just tell us the truth so we can help you."

Adam was only a few feet away but broke into a run and charged at Raine. "Stop saying I murdered my family!"

Adam threw a wild punch at Raine, who was able to dodge it fairly easily. Adam went sailing past them and stumbled onto the ground when he tried to turn around. Raine turned and squared at him. Sommers disappeared into the darkness.

"I don't want to fight you," Raine said. "I want to help you. But I need you to tell me the truth." He really hoped Sarah was hiding in the dark somewhere, listening to everything.

Adam laughed. "You're a lawyer. You don't care about the truth."

Raine frowned at him. "That hurts, Adam."

"I'll give you something that hurts!" Adam shouted, and he charged Raine again.

Raine couldn't avoid Adam a second time, and Adam grabbed him in a bear hug around the waist. Raine punched down on the back of Adam's head until he finally released his grasp, but when he did, he popped straight up and head-butted Raine in the chin. Raine bit his tongue and stumbled backward from the force. Blood started to leak out of the corner of his mouth. Before he could fully regain his senses, Adam threw a punch at his head. It wasn't well aimed and bounced off Raine's forehead, but it added to the stars he was still seeing from the headbutt. Raine lowered himself into a crouch and tried to see where Adam would be coming from next.

"Behind you!" Sommers shouted, but too late.

Adam tackled Raine from behind, sending them both to the ground and skidding toward the building's edge. Raine could feel the cold wind swirling around them.

"Adam, please stop." Raine tried to sound calm. "You don't want to hurt your lawyer. I can help you through this, but you're going to have to take responsibility for your actions."

Adam climbed fully onto Raine's back and threw a flurry of punches against the back of his head. "Stop! Saying! I! Killed! My! Family!"

Raine twisted his body and pushed himself off the floor with all of his strength. That sent Adam tumbling off of him, and they both scrambled to their feet. Raine and Adam started to slowly circle each other, fists raised. They were only feet from the edge of the building. Raine could taste blood, and his ears were ringing. Adam lunged again. Raine landed a solid right hook to Adam's mouth. Adam fell down, but then stood up again, his face bloody. He lunged again at Raine, and again Raine managed to deliver a blow to the face. Adam grabbed at Raine and pulled them both back down to the ground. They were right at the edge of the building now. Raine landed on his back with Adam sitting on top of him. Raine's head was less than a foot from the open air. Adam raised a fist back to punch Raine, but Raine used the moment to push off the deck again and roll over on top of Adam.

Raine grabbed Adam by the shirt and slammed his head into the floor. That seemed to immobilize his opponent.

Raine raised his own fist, ready to deliver a final blow to the center of Adam's face. "Why won't you just tell me you killed your father and brother?"

Before Adam could answer, Raine felt a blinding pain to the back of his head. He fell forward next to Adam, struggling to maintain consciousness. He knew he needed to get to his feet, but the details as to why were fuzzy. Then he heard a voice.

"Because"—Sarah Harper answered Raine's question—"he didn't kill his father and brother," she said. "I did."

S arah was holding a two-foot-long pipe wrench, the weapon the back of Raine's head had just become acquainted with. One more blow to the head from that thing, and it wouldn't matter if he fell off the building.

"You?" Raine managed to croak. "Why?"

"Well, that wasn't the original plan," she admitted. "The original plan was for Mark and Adam to both sue their father and jointly take over the company. But Mark wouldn't do it. When Adam went ahead anyway and their dad changed his will, I saw an opportunity. Bill loved showing off his buildings. I asked for a tour of Harper Tower, but it needed to be late because of my work. He agreed. Never saw me coming. Nineteen stories straight down. Mark would own everything. I would own everything."

Raine was starting to regain some of his senses, but his head was throbbing so badly he could barely keep his eyes open. He could see just well enough to make out Sarah stepping toward him as she talked, wrench still in hand.

"But then Mark said he didn't want to run the company,"

she went on. "He said he couldn't do it. Not without his daddy. He even wanted to give half the company to Adam again. He was always so weak, so goddamn weak. He was crying—literally crying—over his dead daddy. I'd had enough. I said we should go to where his dad died, pay our last respects. I told him this was exactly where his dad fell from. He asked me how I knew. So I showed him.

"I knew it might be suspicious, pushing him from the same place," Sarah admitted. "But I also knew it would work. And the only way to get Mark to go there was to pretend to pay our respects where his dear ol' dad had fallen from."

She laughed darkly. "But I did it too soon. One day too soon. And so this baboon"—she pointed at the motionless Adam—"got everything. I tried that lawsuit, but I could tell I was going to lose. When Zac told me you were the one thing standing between me and a multimillion-dollar payday, I tried to take you out too. Yes, that was me on the bridge that night. I couldn't believe you survived."

Raine recalled being surprised at the time as well. He had a lot of questions, but not a lot of time. If he could stall her, keep her talking, maybe his head would stop spinning. "Is that why you tried to settle the case? To avoid losing it?"

"Isn't that why anyone settles a lawsuit?" Sarah asked in return.

"I suppose so," Raine agreed. He wasn't feeling stronger fast enough.

"But it wasn't as simple as that," Sarah complained. "I had to trick him. He wasn't going to just sign away half of the company. So I went to him and told him I loved him. I didn't tell him what I'd done, of course. I just said I'd always loved him. I would drop the lawsuit, and we could split everything and run away to Fiji or Bali or wherever he needed to hear to believe me. I was a little surprised at how easily he agreed. But when he told me about the deposit fraud tonight, it made sense that he would want to liquidate the company, too, rather than finish Harper Tower."

Adam started to groan as he regained consciousness. Raine was out of time. Sarah would want to finish him off before Adam could witness what happened.

"Oh dear, it looks like our little talk is over," Sarah said. She raised the pipe wrench one last time. "Goodbye, Mr. Raine. Give my regards to my husband."

And then Sommers smashed a three-foot-long metal pipe into the side of Sarah's head. Sarah fell limply to the floor, her wrench rattling safely away across the floor.

Raine wondered if Sarah might actually be dead. He didn't really care. He was just grateful Sommers had been there to make sure he wasn't. "Thanks," he gasped.

"Don't mention it." Sommers reached down and pulled Raine to his feet. "I hate owing people."

# EPILOGUE

Raine stood shirtless in front of his bathroom mirror and surveyed the damage. The cut under his eye had healed, but it was going to leave a small scar. The other cheek was bruised. His lip was still split in the corner. There was a baseball-sized bruise on his upper chest and a smaller one on his ribs. And of course, the back of his head had a goose egg and a dozen stitches.

He splashed some water on his face, gingerly patted it dry, and returned to bed.

Sawyer rolled over and put her head on his chest. "That's a hell of a war story. I'm glad you're not dead."

Raine laughed. It made his ribs hurt. "Thanks. Me too."

"And that lady didn't die either?" Sawyer asked. "The one Rebecca brained with the wrench?"

"No, she survived," Raine answered. "Although she might wish she hadn't. She's going to serve back-to-back sentences for murder one. She'll die in prison."

"And your client, he's going away for a long time too, right?"

"Oh, definitely," Raine said. "A few dozen counts of fraud. He'll be in prison for about a decade."

"Who gets the company?" Sawyer asked, absently running a finger down his arm.

Raine shrugged. "I'm not sure. Adam still inherited it, but he can't run it from prison. And all of those depositors will need to get reimbursed, so it'll probably go bankrupt and get put into some kind of receivership until the court can figure out what to do. Rebecca is already working with the majority of the depositors to find new properties to buy."

"At her standard commission, of course." Sawyer laughed.

"Of course," Raine agreed with a smile.

Sawyer looked up at him. "And you got the girl."

He had to smile at that.

"Although that Ethan guy probably still wants to kick your ass," she said.

"Yeah." Raine supposed that was true.

"And that jerk attorney really is dating your ex, huh?"

Raine sighed. "Apparently so."

Sawyer propped herself up on her elbow and patted Raine's chest. "Still, overall, I'd say you ended up winning."

Raine considered his bruised and beaten body and the broken bodies at the base of Harper Tower.

"I don't know about that," he said, "but I survived."

# WE HOPE YOU ENJOYED THIS BOOK

If you could spend a moment to write an honest review on Amazon, no matter how short, we would be extremely grateful. They really do help readers discover new authors.

# ABOUT THE AUTHOR

Stephen Penner is an author, artist, and attorney from Seattle. He has written over 25 novels and specializes in courtroom thrillers known for their unexpected twists and candid portrayal of the justice system. Stephen began his legal career as a criminal defense attorney, appearing in federal, state, and municipal courts throughout the State of Washington. After several years, Stephen 'switched sides' and became a prosecutor. He has been practicing criminal law for nearly 30 years, working his way up from misdemeanor offenses, to felonies, and finally to homicides. He has conducted over 100 trials and draws on his extensive experience to infuse his writing with realism and insight. In his spare time, Stephen enjoys painting, drawing, and spending time with his family.

---

Visit Stephen Penner on his website:
www.stephenpenner.com

# ALSO BY STEPHEN PENNER

*Rain City Legal Thriller Series*

Burden of Proof

Trial By Jury

The Survival Rule

Made in United States
North Haven, CT
05 January 2024